4

The Hairdresser
of Harare

MODERN
African
Writing
from Ohio University Press

Ghirmai Negash, General Editor
Laura Murphy, Series Editor

This series brings the best African writing to an international audience. These groundbreaking novels, memoirs, and other literary works showcase the most talented writers of the African continent. The series also features works of significant historical and literary value translated into English for the first time. Moderately priced, the books chosen for the series are well crafted, original, and ideally suited for African studies classes, world literature classes, or any reader looking for compelling voices of diverse African perspectives.

Books in the series are published with support from the Ohio University National Resource Center for African Studies.

Welcome to Our Hillbrow
  A Novel of Postapartheid
  South Africa
Phaswane Mpe
ISBN: 978-0-8214-1962-5

Dog Eat Dog: A Novel
Niq Mhlongo
ISBN: 978-0-8214-1994-6

After Tears: A Novel
Niq Mhlongo
ISBN: 978-0-8214-1984-7

From Sleep Unbound
Andrée Chedid
ISBN: 978-0-8040-0837-2

On Black Sisters Street: A Novel
Chika Unigwe
ISBN: 978-0-8214-1992-2

Paper Sons and Daughters
  Growing Up Chinese in South Africa
Ufrieda Ho
ISBN: 978-0-8214-2020-1

The Conscript
  A Novel of Libya's Anticolonial War
Gebreyesus Hailu
ISBN: 978-0-8214-2023-2

Thirteen Cents: A Novel
K. Sello Duiker
ISBN: 978-0-8214-2036-2

Sacred River: A Novel
Syl Cheney-Coker
ISBN: 978-0-8214-2056-0 (hardcover)
  978-0-8214-2137-6 (paperback

491 Days: Prisoner Number 1323/69
Winnie Madikizela-Mandela
ISBN: 978-0-8214-2102-4 (hardcover)
  978-0-8214-2101-7 (paperback)

The Hairdresser of Harare
Tendai Huchu
ISBN: 978-0-8214-2162-8 (hardcover)
  978-0-8214-2163-5 (paperback)

The Hairdresser
of Harare

Tendai Huchu

Ohio University Press   Athens

Ohio University Press, Athens, Ohio 45701
ohioswallow.com

© Tendai Huchu, 2010

Printed in the United States of America
Ohio University Press books are printed on acid-free paper ⊗ ™

First published in 2010 by Weaver Press
Box A1922, Avondale, Harare
Second edition 2011

Cover design by Joey Hi-Fi

This novel is a work of fiction and a product of the author's
imagination. The author's use of actual names and places is not
intended to change the entirely fictional character of the work.
Any likenesses to persons living is purely coincidental.

24 23 22 21 20 19 18 17 16 15   5 4 3 2 1

ISBNS:
978-0-8214-2162-8 (hardcover)
978-0-8214-2163-5 (paperback)

TENDAI HUCHU was born in 1982 in Bindura, Zimbabwe. He attended Churchill High School in Harare and then went to the University of Zimbabwe to study Mining Engineering in 2001. He dropped out in the middle of the first semester when he discovered that the maths had more letters and symbols than it had numbers. Tendai has a great love of literature, in particular the nineteenth century Russian novel. He is now a qualified podiatrist and lives in Edinburgh, Scotland.

One

I knew there was something not quite right about Dumi the very first time I ever laid eyes on him. The problem was, I just couldn't tell what it was. Thank God for that.

There was a time that I was reputed to be the best hairdresser in Harare, which meant the best in the whole country. Amai Ndoro was the fussiest customer to ever grace a salon and she would not let any ordinary *kiya-kiya* touch her hair. Having sampled all the salons in Harare – and rejected them all – she settled on ours. The fussiest customer was also the largest motor mouth and gossip-monger. Once she was our client, we never needed to advertise again, as long as we kept her happy. That was my job and why Mrs Khumalo paid me the highest wage.

Khumalo Hair and Beauty Treatment Salon was in the Avenues, a short walking distance from the city centre. We did hair but never any beauty treatments. In any case I doubt any of us knew how to. There was a rusty metal sign painted white with black lettering on the front gate that pointed to our establishment. The rust, accumulated over several rainy seasons, had eaten away so much of the sign that only Khu—l-, a drawing of a lady with a huge afro and an arrow still showed. Our customers didn't need it, the directions were simple.

'Go up from Harare Gardens, skip two roads, take a left, skip another road and look for the blue house on your right, not the green one, and you're there.' You'd have to be a nincompoop to miss it.

The front section of the house, which once served as a lounge, was converted into an internet café with a dozen or so computers. You could hear the fans humming and the shriek of the dialler from the pavement across the road. Their prices weren't too bad either, compared to those at Eastgate or Ximex Mall. The rest of the main house was used by the Khumalo family, all thirteen of them.

Our salon was at the back in what used to be the boy's kaya, servant's quarters. From across the yard, the fragrant aroma of relaxers, dyes, shampoos and a dozen other chemicals hit you. The smell merged with the dust from the driveway and left something in your nostrils that you couldn't shake off until the next time you caught a cold.

The building had been crudely extended. A wall had been knocked down to the left and concrete blocks hastily laid to add another seven metres. Such architectural genius had left us with a hybrid building, the likes of which you could only find if you looked hard. The right of the building was constructed of proper burnt bricks, professionally built in every respect. You could see the dividing line where the cheap concrete blocks had been used. Aesthetics aside, we were all grateful for the accommodation though it rattled a little during heavy storms.

Each morning I was greeted by Agnes with, "Sisi Vimbai, you're late again. Customers are waiting." Mrs Khumalo's eldest daughter held the keys and opened shop.

I would make a sound like 'Nxii' with my lips and walk in without greeting the cow. I hated her, she hated me twice as much and so long as mummy wasn't in, there was no need to pretend otherwise. Everyone knew I was the goose that laid the golden eggs. If I left, half the customers would follow me. In any case letting them wait made them realise how lucky they were to be served at all, so I was actually doing the business a favour.

There were three other hairdressers, Memory, Patricia and Yolanda plus Charlie Boy, our barber, who always came in smelling of Chibuku. The salon was my personal fiefdom and I was queen bee. I would throw my handbag on the floor underneath the cashier's desk and boil myself a cup of tea.

"There is a new style I want you to do for me." How often have I heard these words, usually followed by a folded picture torn from some glossy American magazine.

"*Nxii*, I can do that easily, it's just the style for you!" I always indulged them with a white lie.

There's only one secret to being a successful hairdresser and I've never withheld it from anyone. 'Your client should leave the salon feeling like a white woman.' Not Coloured, not Indian, not Chinese. I have told this to everyone who's ever asked me and what they all want to know is how d'you make someone feel like a white woman. Sigh, yawn, scratch.

The answer is simple, 'whiteness is a state of mind'.

Mrs Khumalo understands this and that's why she would never fire me. The other girls don't understand it and that's why Patricia was fired. The stupid girl got pregnant less than six months into the job, so, of course, Mrs K. had no choice Hairdressers are there to sell an image and that image is not pushing a football in your belly. Suddenly we had a vacancy. Little did I know that this small twist of fate would cost me my crown.

Two

The grapevine is an amazing thing. Patricia had only been sacked for two days but the phone was already ringing off the hook. Each caller had somehow heard that we had a vacancy and they were ready to start straight away. I must have answered a dozen calls before I refused to take another one. Agnes sat in a corner reading a magazine. She only ever worked when her mother was in.

I was doing a perm for a fat customer when the phone rang again.

"You're doing nothing, can you answer the phone?" I shouted. If she'd been my daughter, I would have slapped her.

She got up slowly and went to the desk.

"Helloow," she said like a person on a toilet, but the caller had already hung up.

"Sit by the phone and write all their names and details into that exercise book." This girl was so lazy, you had to spell everything out.

"Don't you tell me what to do! You're just a worker. One day you're going to get fired too and I'll be answering calls for your job."

'Stupid girl, if I go your mother will be out of business' was what I wanted to say, but we had customers. My ugly one wriggled uncomfortably. I could tell she was not feeling white yet, but I was so angry I couldn't have cared less.

Wearing a green Nigerian bou bou, which hugged the contours of her amply fed body, Mrs Khumalo came in later that day kicking the dust off her feet. The government had given her a few hectares on a farm thirty kilometres down the Mazowe Road so she spent a good amount of her time there. It was where Mr Khumalo now lived permanently, since they'd also been given the farm manager's house.

"Agnes, get me a glass of water." Her high-pitched voice echoed round the room. Whenever she spoke, it was so loudly that I assumed she thought we were all deaf. She drank the water in one gulp and placed the glass on the desk. Behind her puffed eyelids, her tiny eyes surveyed the salon and seemed disappointed that there weren't more customers in the queue.

"Makadini henyu, Mrs Khumalo?" my fat customer said.

"Matilda, I'd heard you'd left us for Easy Touch Salon." Mrs K. never forgot any of her customers' names, a trait that I wished I shared.

"They're cheaper but they don't know what they're doing." Fat Matilda answered.

"Everyone who goes there comes back. I hear horror stories about people's hair snapping off." It was an exaggeration, but destroying a competitor's reputation was all part of the game. Easy Touch, in turn, spread a rumour that we were wenches who wanted to steal our customers' husbands. It must have scared some women off because we were all beautiful except for Agnes who shared her mother's toady-ish shape. Neither mother nor daughter had necks. Shame.

It was left to me to tell Mrs Khumalo about the calls we'd been getting for the vacancy. This was something else I admired about her. Had it been another person, they would have looked for a relative to fill the position, but not Mrs Khumalo. She wanted the best people working for her.

I put Fatty in the dryer in the centre of the room for her perm to set before I could take the rollers out. One wall of the salon had the wash-basins, the other chairs and a third side was reserved for Charlie Boy and his male customers. The dryers were placed in the centre because we didn't have anywhere else to put them. The fourth wall had shelves carrying our stocks, and a large mirror.

"Are any of these girls who've phoned professionals?"

I should have used cotton wool to plug my ears.

"I know two of them personally."

"Which ones?"

I hesitated. I didn't want to recommend someone who turned out to be useless, but if I'd known what was to come I would have pushed for anyone of them, useless or not.

***

A man walked up the drive. The sound of his feet crunched on the pebbles. He hesitantly read the sign to see if he was at the right place.

"Is this Mrs Khumalo's hair salon?"

"Couldn't you read the sign?" Agnes called out. We all laughed like a pack of hyenas. Charlie Boy came to the front, certain he had a customer. I don't know why he was kept on. Very few men came in for a haircut or shave so the barbershop was hardly profitable.

"Come in sonny, I will sort that hair of yours out in no time." Charlie Boy quipped.

The man had an afro. I would have been sad to see it shaved off. Stylish and well kempt, it glistened in the sun, a sure sign that he was using oils. He was about twenty-two with a well-proportioned boyish physique, pleasing to the eye. The black trousers and short-sleeved white shirt made him look like a junior clerk in the civil service.

"I've come to see Mrs Khumalo." His voice was soft yet clear.

"What do you want?" she asked.

He took a timid step and stopped at the doorway to look around the salon and its many American hairstyle posters that we'd pinned on the walls. His searching eyes studied everything from our stocks to the seats. I took fatty Matilda out from under the dryer and led her to the cash desk. The young man could not take his eyes off her. Men want their women big and round, *mutefetefe*. Her voluptuous buttocks bounced around as if to mock me.

"I said, 'what do you want?'" Mrs Khumalo snapped him out of his trance.

"I heard that you had a vacancy."

"So you want something for your sister or cousin maybe. Tell me

6

her name and her qualifications."

"I need the job myself."

Agnes let out a squeak, and I began to laugh.

"Young man, d'you think I am looking for a garden-boy? I want a hairdresser." Mrs Khumalo laughed. She sounded like a pig, much like her daughter. The young man turned as if to go.

"I can do the job Mrs Khumalo, if you give me a chance."

"Don't be stupid. We mustn't waste each other's time. Go away." If you weren't putting money into her till, Mrs K. had no reason to be nice to you. These were difficult times and jobs were scarce but I'd never thought that men might try to get a woman's job. A male hairdresser, who'd ever heard of such a thing? But instead of leaving, the young man stepped into the shop towards Matilda who was counting out her money. She grasped her handbag tightly between her breasts. The man flicked her hair with his hand.

"Hey what do you think you are doing?" Charlie Boy shouted. Even an unlikely male figure can be some protection against Harare's bold thieves.

"Trust me, sister. This is your chance to help me." The man said, his voice as soft as running water. "Your hair was set beautifully, but the style she's given you is not for you." He picked up a fine-toothed comb from the table and ran it through her hair. "You have a round face, so instead of these curls we need to layer it so that it flows with the smooth contours of your face." He worked briskly with his comb, then took a pair of scissors to trim the ends.

My heart was pounding with rage. It had taken me an hour and a half to do that style and he dared to say that I'd got it wrong. The customer is always king. I'd done the style she asked for.

"Hey you…" Charlie Boy moved forward.

"No, please let him finish Mrs Khumalo." Matilda said.

Our boss was silent as she watched him with a quiet fascination. If I hadn't known her better, I would have said she seemed amused. The stranger worked quickly like an artist working on a living sculpture. His long slender fingers primed the hair and everyone's eyes were focused on him. A few customers stepped out from under their dryers to watch him work.

Five minutes later he was finished. He put his hands on Matilda's shoulders and made her look in the mirror. She blinked. He picked up a mirror so that she could see the back of her head as well.

"What do you think?" he asked.

"Sweet Jesus, I look like Naomi Campbell." Matilda's body was trembling with excitement.

"You see what I meant about the layers."

"This is wonderful. Please give me your phone number."

That is when Mrs Khumalo stepped in. She'd seen enough. She gently took Matilda by the hand and ushered her to the door. "Don't worry, you'll find him here next time you come."

The young man said that his name was Dumisani. Mrs Khumalo didn't care. She took his details and told him that he was to start work the following Monday.

Three

The house that I lived in was far bigger than anything I could have dreamt of. It stood in Eastlea, a low-density suburb, home to the middle classes where people like me passed through carrying large baskets on our heads. A neighbourhood with an English name is a good neighbourhood. There are exceptions to the rule of course like Highfields or Hatcliffe, high-density areas. So to make the distinction we *Shonarized* these names: Highfields became *Highfiridzi*; Hatcliffe was *Hatikirifi*.

It was natural and instinctive that when we pronounced the names of really plush neighbourhoods, like Borrowdale, with its sprawling mansions, we spoke in a nasal tone to try and sound more English.

I had Tony Blair to thank for living in Eastlea in my elder brother's house. A four-bedroomed bungalow with a red roof set on an acre of land. The lawn was slowly turning into desert but for the weeds, which had taken over. The flower-beds, which once boasted many foreign botanical specimens, were also wilting. Only sturdy geraniums and self-seeding marigolds remained giving some colour. A Durawall surrounded the property and shielded our shameful garden from prying eyes.

The backyard was a different story. There we had eight beds of cultivated vegetables: rape and tomatoes, onions and carrots, cabbages and pumpkins. There was a guava tree in the corner by the servant's quarters. The peach tree had long since died and been used for firewood. A stump remained as a sort of inanimate memorial. One day we would uproot it and burn it too.

When I reached home, my daughter Chiwoniso was red, the same colour as the soil in this part of town. Together with her little school friends she was wallowing in mud.

"Get out of there all of you!" I shouted.

"Mama!" they said in unison and came speeding towards me.

"Get away from me."

I was wearing a white dress. I don't know what's wrong with kids these days. They don't listen. They mobbed me anyway and soon I was looking like them in my soiled dress. If only they knew how hard it was to wash out soil stains. I took some sweets from my bag and gave them two each. My heart warmed when they clapped their hands to thank me.

"Make sure you all go to your homes by six o'clock." They were too young to tell the time but they knew to leave just as the sun began to set.

The house was empty except for Sisi Maidei, my house-girl. I'd grown up in a tiny two-bedroomed house in Tafara sharing the floor with five other girls. I was unused to space and the privacy. There was never any peace when I was growing up; I was always surrounded by the sound of laughter and insistent chatter. In a way I missed it, but I had learnt to love my own space.

"*Maswera sei?*" said Sisi Maidei.

"*Taswera maswerawo.*"

I told her to make me some Tanganda tea. My throat was dry. I sat down on the sofa and relaxed. I had been on my feet all day and my arches were very sore. I rubbed them to ease the pain. Outside the window the children were back in their mud hole, their joyful faces wrapped in the innocence of childhood. I was here to protect them. I had no desire for Chiwoniso to have the same childhood that I'd endured.

"Here's your tea."

"Thank you." I took a sip, "You always put too much sugar. What's wrong with you? Do you think I buy it with paper?"

The stupid girl just stood there looking at me until I dismissed her with a wave of my hand. That was the problem with these rural girls, they lacked common sense. I knew I had to replace her, but not with someone too clever. The city girls would steal from you at the first chance they had. It was getting harder and harder to find a good house-girl.

Chiwoniso entered the house, her tiny feet leaving footprints on the floor.

I told Maidei to clear up and took my daughter to the bathroom.

"But Mama, I don't want to bath." She squirmed but I was firm and held her tightly.

"If you keep wriggling like this there will be no more sweets for you." She fell still, her tiny mind debating the situation, perhaps weighing if one bath was worth losing sweets over. Her face contorted in anguish.

"Don't worry, I'll bath with you," I said. Her smile shone like tiny moonbeams on my face. I kissed her, we were friends once more.

One day when she grows older she will understand why I insist on bathing her myself every evening. Only six years old and in her first year in primary school, she could not possibly know that I was checking for any signs of abuse. I knew I was being paranoid but the *Herald* was always full of stories about abused children … it seems that nowadays whether it's AIDS or *muti* or just the way things are, children become the victims. Sylvia once told me that the Child Abuse Clinic at Harare Hospital was seeing a hundred kids a week and that was just the tip of the iceberg. The only way that was going to happen to Chiwoniso was over my dead body and even then, my *ngozi* would still have something to say about that.

Maidei was outside cooking supper on a three-plate hearth we'd recently built to save electricity. The costs had gone up again and I was two months behind with payments. The security light outside shone on her as she adjusted the logs to kindle the fire. Her strong hands worked rhythmically as she stirred the pots. A machine of flesh designed for a lifetime of servitude. The one thing I admired about her was her ability to do work quietly and uncomplainingly. She did the yard and the garden as well because I could scarcely afford to hire a garden-boy. In that moment I felt myself thinking maybe I shouldn't get rid of her after all.

Supper was sadza with *matemba* with some pumpkin leaves mixed with tomatoes and onions, cooked in beef fat to give them more flavour. The smell was heavenly but I had to add more salt. Clearly there was still a lot to teach this girl. Chiwoniso hated *matemba*, so I indulged her and let her have lacto with her sadza.

"Tell me about your day at school," I said.

She began a convoluted tale about her teacher, other students, class and Lord knows what else. It made very little sense but I marvelled at her fluent English. It rolled from her little tongue sounding natural, not forced like mine.

She went to bed late. It was Friday, so she didn't have to get up early. Maidei went to bed once she'd done the dishes. Chiwoniso asked me to tell her a story like I'd once done so so long ago. I kissed her on the forehead and covered her with a blanket wishing that it would always be this way.

Then I made my way around the house checking all the doors and windows. We had a latch on every door and burglar bars on all the windows but I knew that even this was sometimes not enough. The thieves in Harare worked 24/7 and a house full of women made for easy pickings. I wheeled the TV into my bedroom just in case. A house just up the street had recently been burgled and they'd lost everything, even the light bulbs. What was worse was that the family remained fast asleep, waking up to find themselves naked on the floor. There were rumours that burglars were blowing some sort of sleeping powder through the air vents but no one ever said what the powder was or where they got it from.

Finally, I went to bed and stared at the ceiling trying not to think how this house had driven a wedge between me and my family.

Four

I was late again for work on Monday. This time Mrs Khumalo herself greeted me.

"This is a business, Vimbai! Customers are waiting and you're modelling," she called out, as I made my way up the driveway. Agnes sniggered as I quickened my pace.

"I'm sorry, but the kombis from Kamfinsa were all full."

I wondered what she was doing in so early. She seemed to be nervous as she stared at the slow procession of cars going down the road. I accompanied Sylvia, one of our regulars, to the basin. No time for tea when the boss is here. One day I will have enough money for my own salon, I thought, as I ran my fingers through her hair. Sylvia was a nurse at Parirenyatwa and people in the medical field were always handy to know. Maybe she would help me to jump the queue one day. Though God forbid I should get sick.

Sylvia's hair was straight except in the nape of her neck where her new curly hair was growing out in its natural state.

"You shouldn't have left it so long before coming in for a retouch. There's a lot of growth in here."

"I know, but money is hard to come by these days."

"Don't worry, I'll give you a discount today." Mrs Khumalo cast a sharp glance my way and I quickly added, "This is your tenth consecutive visit so you deserve it."

There was something wrong today and I could feel the tension in the air. It took me a while to realise what the problem was.

"Agnes, go and look up the street," said Mrs Khumalo.

"That's why you shouldn't take these people in from the street," quipped Charlie Boy. He had a customer, a man having a punky haircut, like he was still in the eighties.

I wriggled my nose as the Revlon relaxer worked its magic on Sylvia's hair.

"Make sure you tell me when your scalp starts tingling," I told her. She knew the risks well. I remembered the first time she'd come in, her scalp was scabbed where she'd been burnt by Glen-T, that horrible local stuff. It was weeks before she could have her hair done professionally. She'd stayed loyal ever since.

Agnes returned shaking her head.

"Did you look properly?" Mrs Khumalo asked.

"Yes, Mama, there's no one."

Mrs Khumalo looked downcast. She threw the cashbook on the table, picked up her cellphone. She couldn't get a signal so she stepped outside and hovered around trying until she got one.

"Dumisani, where are you? It's Mrs Khumalo, please call me when you get this message, we are tired of waiting for you." She hung up the phone and sighed. "Maybe he has a problem." We all cast each other conspiratorial looks. This was not the boss we knew. How could she be so tolerant with someone not showing up, and on his first day, when we all knew there were hundreds of hairdressers looking for work. Mrs K. rolled up her sleeves and asked the next customer to come forward. In Zimbabwe you have to learn to be a jack of all trades: Mrs Khumalo was a hairdresser, farmer, trader, IT consultant, you name it, she did it.

Only Agnes had the guts to ask her about this newfound blast of tolerance.

"What's so special about him? We can get someone else."

"There's something about that boy. I saw the way he styled Matilda's hair. He knows how to do the job better than some of you who've been here years." That stung. Who was she referring to – me or the other girls?

I inserted the latest CD by Papa Wemba, my favourite Congolese artist, into the CD player. The salon was not complete without a little Rhumba in the background. Even Mrs Khumalo jiggled her hips in rhythm to the beat and in that instant looked like a sexy young woman again.

"Do you have Kofi Olomide or Kanda Bongoman?" a customer said.

"We have everything you want, one hundred per cent satisfaction guaranteed. Hey *chinja* that CD."

Agnes put Kanda Bongoman on and the customer laughed content. The guitars and the rhythmic beats from the Congo blared out and could be heard in the street. When we wanted to speak, we shouted above the music. 'Hand me that comb. Do this, do that.' The salon came to life.

A boy came in later that morning; he was not much older than my daughter. He wore shorts and a blue T-shirt that was so tight that his belly button showed.

"*MaFreezits,*" he said, lowering the large box that he carried on his unkempt head.

We all bought the frozen popsicles more out of sympathy than because of the heat. He came by every day and sometimes we bought nothing. There were many more like him roaming about the city. I shuddered when I imagined my own child having to leave school and fend for herself. I recalled a time when the city council forced truant kids into school or rounded up street kids and put them in orphanages. Nowadays nobody bothered. None of these high-handed measures had worked anyway.

He thanked us and went on his way. I could see Mrs Khumalo watching him until he was out of sight. Her face showed a mother's concern and helplessness all rolled into one. She already had far too many mouths to feed.

A shiny black Mercedes C-class pulled in. Agnes lowered the volume on the stereo. My heart beat faster. It was our top client. The chauffeur ran round and opened the door for her. I was disappointed she'd not brought her husband with her. He was a nice man who sometimes hung about and chatted while her hair was being done. The lady, who was Minister M___ (after what happened, I could never bring myself to mention her by name) got out and walked towards us. Mrs Khumalo was beside herself ordering Memory to sweep hair from the floor.

Yolanda got a chair ready and stood behind it as the minister made her way in.

"It's so good to see you again."

"How are you? Please seat down." There was a slight tremor in Mrs K.'s voice. She clapped her hands in the traditional fashion and the lady responded in kind.

Minister M____ came in to get her hair done once a month. She had grown up in rural Chivhu, Charter as it was known then, the same area that Mrs Khumalo came from. A lot of people assumed Mrs Khumalo was Ndebele, but actually she was Shona, it was her husband who had the Ndebele roots. The Minister even called her *Vatete*, auntie, because by some conjuring trick they had managed to establish a relationship based on their totems.

Minister M____ had joined the liberation struggle when she was only fourteen. She had trained in Zambia with ZANLA and had fought bravely against the Rhodesian Army. After independence, she entered politics and continued with her schooling. In the late eighties she became a deputy minister and later a full minister. She wore spectacles and had a gap in her teeth, which made it sound like she was whistling when she spoke.

"Vimbai, are you going to do my hair?" She always asked this even though she knew I was the only one allowed to touch her. I left my customer for Yolanda to finish off. "How's Chiwoniso, that's her name isn't it? I wish I'd brought something for her."

"She's fine – you got her name right." It amazed me the way she remembered our names although we were nobodies.

"How's your mother feeling these days?" she asked Memory.

"Much better, but her bones cause her problems when it's raining." The minister nodded sympathetically.

"Is she getting the medicine she needs?"

"Yes, but it's expensive. Things are very difficult these days."

"Go to the pharmacy on Angwa Street. Tell them I sent you and they will give you whatever you need for her. Make sure you take a prescription."

Memory clapped her hands and thanked the minister. Tears formed in her eyes as if she was overwhelmed. The minister pretended not to notice and turned to Yolanda.

"Are you still going to night school?"

"I'm getting ready for my final exams."

"You're a good girl. You'll pass. The country needs educated young people like you. You are the future."

Yolanda bowed her head slightly embarrassed. She was doing A-levels at night school because her parents didn't have the money to send her to a good school. She could have gone to a B-school somewhere in the townships, but she was a classy girl and refused to.

"Who are you?" the minister asked a customer who was sitting in the corner waiting.

The customer seemed surprised that she was being spoken to.

"Me?" she asked. The minister gestured yes patiently. "I am Patience Chidhakwa."

The minister thought for a minute and spoke slowly.

"The Chidhakwas from Buhera?"

"Yes."

"What's your phone number?"

"It is 01135..."

"No, you're supposed to say double nine, nine, two, ten," said Mrs Khumalo referring to an old hit song from the eighties and laughed loudly.

"She is too young to know this." The minister laughed as well. "So Patience, you're my little sister because I have a cousin who is married into your people."

Who would not be pleased to know they were in some way related to the minister? I liked the way she whistle-spoke and carried herself. There was a down-to-earth quality about her; she felt like one of the girls, even though we all knew she was loaded. She spoke with Mrs Khumalo about her farm and encouraged her. When she left, we all felt special even as we stared after her shiny car that lay far beyond our wildest dreams.

Five

The next day Dumisani didn't show up. Nor did he show up on Tuesday or Wednesday. I couldn't understand how anyone could waste such an opportunity – a job was a job these days. After all, we all knew there was 90 per cent unemployment! Mrs Khumalo came into the salon every day looking more downcast with each passing hour.

"Maybe he isn't going to come anymore," she said to no one in particular.

It rained that day and the salon was virtually empty except for one customer who Memory was attending to. I listened to the sound of the raindrops bombarding the roof like a thousand tiny bullets. The sky was grey and it was hard to imagine that behind all those clouds the sun still shone.

"Did you hear the latest about Patricia?" asked Memory, who was as fond of a bit of gossip as all of us.

"Come on, tell us."

"I found out whose pregnancy that was. You'll not believe it."

"I would believe anything of that girl."

"It's Pastor Chasi's child."

"You have to be joking! Pastor Chasi from the New Jerusalem Church? I can't believe it."

"That's what you get from these Pentecostal churches of yours,"

Mrs Khumalo cut in. She was a staunch Catholic and a member of some guild that wore blue uniforms when they went to mass.

"Isn't Pastor Chasi married?"

"He has a wife and two kids."

"Isn't that the church you go to, Vimbai?"

"No, I go to Forward in Faith ministries."

"He's refusing to accept the baby."

It made for a juicy piece of gossip but there was nothing new about the story of a pastor getting one of his flock pregnant. He could easily turn around and say that the Holy Spirit made him do it; but chances were that Patricia would be given some money and told to keep quiet. I had no moral high ground on which to stand in such matters. That's why I generally kept quiet when the girls gossiped about such things.

I was very young when I had Chiwoniso. Her father was a very well-known businessman. Nineteen and unemployed, I was still living with my parents. But one day, coming home from the shops, a car pulled over. I was surprised to see it was Phillip Mabayo, a flamboyant, good-looking man who was often on TV and had his name splashed in the newspapers almost daily. He was in his late thirties but had made enough money for twenty lifetimes. How? It was better not to ask. He was driving a red Ford pick-up, left-hand-drive. It was the only one in the country. I thought he wanted to ask me for directions when he rolled down his window. The street was full of people and so I was so surprised when he said,

"Girl you're so beautiful. Get in. Let's go for a ride."

"Leave me alone," I said, embarrassed. Luckily our house was just around the corner and I ran to our gate. I may have been innocent but I wasn't stupid; I'd heard about Sugar Daddies!

When I told my sister what had happened she said I was an idiot. I didn't care. I had a boyfriend, the same age as me and even though he owned nothing, I loved him with the deluded passion that only youth can offer. A few days later, a neighbour's child came over and asked for me. He gave me a cellphone and said it was for me. I asked who it was from and he said a man had given it to him.

"Don't be a fool. Take it." my sister said.

It was a silver Nokia with a colour screen, ready to use, with a sim-card installed. For the first time in my life, I had my own phone. But it was not long before I knew who'd given it to me. My suspicions were confirmed when the phone rang and there was a man on the end. I remember my mother asking where I had got a phone from as I left the room to take the call. My sister mumbled some excuse on my behalf.

"Who is it?"

"It's Phillip. Do you like your new phone or would you have preferred a Motorola."

I stuttered over my words.

"Aren't you even going to thank me?"

"Thanks."

Ice broken, we spoke for about half an hour until he said he had to go. No one in my family said a thing and I chose to assume I had their approval. Each time he called, we spoke for longer and then he asked me out for lunch. I had never been taken out before and I said yes.

We arranged to meet on the corner beyond the shops. There was no way I could have him pick me up at my parents' house. He was driving a long silver BMW. I had never sat in a car like it and eased myself timidly onto the seat beside him as he helped me with my seatbelt. The aircon hummed in the cool interior and I was amazed by how much space there was. Those days he smiled a lot as we listened to soul music from the nineties. The car hit potholes on the patchy road but I hardly felt them. It was so comfortable inside.

"This is what being in Germany is like," he said. "Have you ever been to Europe?"

"I have a brother in the UK."

"That's very good, is he in the BBC?"

"No he does other jobs."

"I meant British Bottom Cleaner." He apologised immediately when he saw that I did not like my brother to be insulted, even though I was sure he'd said it in jest.

"So you said there were six kids in your family. Which one is he?"

"He's the fifth."

"And you're the youngest of course. That's why you two are so close. Maybe when I next go there I should pay him a visit. Where does he stay?"

"Slough."

"Oh that place! I have a flat in central London. I could have let him use it for free."

He was an experienced man, who'd seen the world and I was just a guileless girl; the furthest I'd ever been was Murombedzi, where my grandmother lived. We went to Nardo's and he asked me what I wanted. Even though I'd read the menu, I could not bring myself to choose, so he ordered rice and peri-peri chicken for me. The rich spices gave the food more flavour than the bland sadza and veg, which was our daily staple at home. I'd never used a fork and knife, but Phillip wasn't bothered if I used a spoon for my rice and my hands for the meat. I remember thinking to myself, 'This is the high-life.'

I was a shy person those days. It's not possible to be innocent without being shy. Phillip did most if not all of the talking. He enjoyed talking about his businesses. I loved it when he spoke about stocks and shares, things that I had no knowledge of. It was the opening up of a whole new world for me. He looked at me as if I was the most precious thing in the universe and ignored the stream of people who said 'Hello Mr Mabayo,' as they passed by. I could feel the stares of envious women with heavy make-up and fashionable clothes boring through me, as they wondered how a township girl like me had bagged the famous Phillip Mabayo. But I hadn't bagged him. Phillip knew that I had a boyfriend and he said he respected that. He just wanted to be friends.

"Do you want to go to my house?" he asked.

"No."

"That's fine." He looked at the watch and said, "In any case I have to head back to work. I won't be able to take you home. I'm sure you'll be okay catching a kombi, won't you? From his wallet he fished out a wad of cash and handed it to me without even bothering to count it. In those days it was still possible to carry money in a wallet.

"This is too much."

"Oh really?" He seemed genuinely surprised. "I wouldn't know how much a kombi costs anyway. Use the change to buy yourself something nice."

This amount of money could feed my whole family for a month.

I told my envious sister all about it and she wished I had brought her a piece of chicken. We waited for him to call but he didn't phone me that night. I lay on the floor surrounded by bodies. My mind was in flux. Once you've had a little nibble of this world, you can't help but want more. I reflected on my boyfriend, who came to see me wearing flip-flops, and thought of Phillip with the world at his feet. It took a while to fall asleep with all these thoughts swirling in my head.

I bought new clothes with the money that he gave me. I had my hair done and wore make-up. No one at home asked me where I was getting the money from. Baba remained silent and mother remarked on how lovely I looked. Phillip got me a new phone, one with a camera. I gave my old one, which was barely a month old, to my sister. Looking back, it was all so romantic. I was being wooed for the first time in my life. I stopped seeing my boyfriend and did not answer the desperate love notes he sent me. Phillip began to tell me how much he loved me. I received texts and late-night phone calls. That man had a way with words. I had fallen for him, but I couldn't have known that lurking underneath his posh exterior lay a monster. There was a heavy price to pay for my naivety.

Six

The phone rang and Mrs Khumalo leapt up as fast as her heavy frame would allow. It was the call she'd been waiting for.

"...I am sorry to hear that... where are you... I see... do you need more time... that's good... are you sure because there is no rush... no problem see you tomorrow."

A huge smile lit up her face. She looked out into the rain and asked if there were any customers with appointments in the book. There were none.

"You can all go home when you want to. Agnes and I will be just fine. That boy Dumisani is starting work tomorrow. His friend died and because he has no family in Zimbabwe, he had to arrange for the body to be shipped to Canada all by himself. I knew there had to be something very wrong, he looks too responsible for any nonsense."

I had the day off on Friday because of my brother Robert's memorial.

Taking a kombi home is always a daunting task. The first problem is getting on one, especially from Samora Machel where I took mine, just beyond Fourth Street below the grey multi-storey coffin that is the government department responsible for tax revenues. There were a lot of kombis but they seemed to spend most of the time queuing for petrol – that is, when it could be found – and stalled when they had it. The few petrol stations that had fuel only accepted foreign currency or coupons though it was still technically illegal to carry out transactions in foreign currency.

There was a sizeable group of us waiting as cars trickled past on the dual carriageway. It was rush hour but they moved ever so slowly in an attempt to save fuel. I tried hard not to think about the brief period in my life when I moved about in a car. Some drivers stopped to pick people up. We called it piracy and it was illegal. They all seemed to be going towards the affluent northern suburbs.

"Can you tell me what time it is?" a man in an oversized cheap suit asked me. He looked like a civil servant.

"Half past five."

"Thanks." He drew closer. "You look like someone I've met before."

I ignored him; being chatted up at the bus stop was nothing new. He persisted. "Do you go to Christ Ministries?"

He looked like a typical nice guy. It's a pity he didn't know that I hadn't been in a relationship for six years and had no intentions of changing that. Men didn't appeal to me any more. They couldn't be trusted.

"You think you're special, but you're not even beautiful," he finally volunteered. Getting abused was nothing new. "You'll die without a man."

A kombi came by and I jumped in, glad to escape. Men don't take rejection so well. It's like they're raised expecting that they can have whatever they want. I was sandwiched between other bodies and could hardly breathe. The seat designed for three was filled with four people with the *hwindi* leaning over our laps because there was no space for him. Crowding to maximise profits. The smell of sweat and bad breath was overpowering. Even after a lifetime of experience, it was impossible to enjoy this type of travel. I can vaguely recall a time when we had buses that ran to a timetable in Harare. The kombi had no timetable and observed so few rules that you had to pray you'd reach your destination because quite often they'd just decide to change their route leaving you stranded.

The one advantage of the kombi was its willingness to stop anywhere. I dropped off right in front of a 'No Stopping' sign and went home.

***

The lively bustle of the townships can never be replicated in the low-density areas. I passed my old high school where I'd spectacularly flunked my O-levels. It was break time and the children were kicking up the dust, playing football. The streets were full of people moving in both directions. Some carried hoes to tend their fields by the roadside, always fearful that the city council would come and slash their 'illegal' crops.

A cobbler sat on a street corner. Business was brisk. Ever since the government's Look-East policy, the country had been flooded by cheap Chinese shoes that only lasted a dozen steps before falling apart at the seams. We didn't throw away shoes. But to be on the safe side, he was also selling *manyetera*, stocky sandals made of old tyres, ugly but guaranteed to last. I had a pair at home myself.

There were vendors selling freezits, *maputi,* maize cobs, fruit, eggs, and vegetables. It seemed as though there were more vendors than purchasers. With no jobs available everyone tried to sell something, just to eke out a living. Almost every second house had a wooden shack near the gate: tuck shops, only a little classier than the vendors with their makeshift stalls. Within each was a family member, no doubt a minor, looking bored, and waiting for the very occasional customers to dribble in.

I saw the backyard salons where I had learnt my trade growing up. They were brisk businesses and catered for women who could not go to upmarket salons like Mrs Khumalo's. They used cheap chemicals but their work competed with the best of us in town.

"Sisi Vimbai, long time no see," my old school friend, Fortunate, called out to me.

"I've been busy *sha.*" I offered to shake her hand but she embraced me instead.

"You're too good for us now."

"It's not like that."

"Then you have a new man. Tell us."

"I'm still single and not searching. What have you been doing?"

"I have a daughter as well now."

"*Makorokoto.*" I reached into my purse and gave her some money. She took it readily and thanked me.

"Who's the father?"

"John Chimuti." The name rang a bell and I knew instantly that she would be joining the ranks of the many used girls who lived with their parents when the father had done a runner. It was not so long ago that I'd been in her shoes.

We parted ways and I plodded on. The air hung thick with woodsmoke. No one could afford paraffin, if you could find it that is. A lot of people greeted me as I walked along. I felt an atmosphere of friendliness, violence, innovation, poverty, joy but the one thing that hung over everything else was despair; an air of hopelessness as if everyone was in a pit that they could not climb out of. I knew that feeling all too well. It's like seeing a plane high up in the sky and knowing that you will never be on it.

I reached my parents' house and stood hesitantly at the gate. I wanted to walk in as confidently as I used to but I found myself rattling the chain at the gate and hoping that someone would invite me in. Two dogs, Plato and Aristotle, ran toward me growling but quickly began to wag their tails and bark excitedly when they recognised me. The house was the same pink bungalow with an asbestos roof that I'd grown up in. I've heard that asbestos can make you sick, but nearly every house in the neighbourhood had an asbestos roof. A curtain was drawn open and I could see someone peeping out.

The sun pounded on my head as I waited. No one came to open the gate for me. I rattled the chain again and still no one came. I wanted to walk away but my heart yearned to be there for Robert's memorial. I called out to them to open the gate.

"Go away!"

The words stung like a bullet. I had half expected this reception. There would be no reconciliation, even at Robert's grave. I would have to go on my own.

"Vimbai, we weren't expecting you to come."

"He was my brother too," I said.

"All the same after everything that's happened..." This was my brother Fungai, the third born in our family, suddenly appearing from the tuckshop round the corner carrying a small bag of maize meal. "I don't think they're going to let you in."

"I don't care," I lied. "I'm going to his grave anyway."

"That's good. You know I said I was neutral in this whole issue; but I wish you guys could talk. We are family."

"You try telling them that."

Fungai walked me back to the bus station. He fancied himself a philosopher and had even managed a year at the UZ, which he passed with flying colours. That's why the dogs had the weird names of men who he said were great philosophers. Robert had been paying his fees, but after he'd died Fungai had to drop out of university because there was no money. We chatted about everything except the cause of the dispute. Fungai told me how he'd established a philosophy group that met every afternoon to discuss everything under the sun. I promised him that one day I would come to see them if he promised to visit me at the house some time.

The wounds were still fresh, passions still high. It was disappointing that as a family we could not rise above what was a material dispute and come together for this memorial. I wondered just how Robert would feel if he were looking down on us witnessing this ugliness. It could not have been what he had intended.

Seven

The cemetery was much bigger than I remembered it. It was called Mbudzi, meaning goat. I never found out why. It was only twelve months since we'd buried Robert and the cemetery was twice as large. The rows of earth heaps stretched into the distance. Beyond them was bush. The earth was black, for the grass had been burnt in a random fire that no one had tried to stop. Ash rose high in the sky whenever the wind blew and snagged in your clothes. The dry trees bowed low seemingly resigned that soon they too would be chopped down to make way for more graves.

A few of the graves were covered in concrete. Fewer had tombstones on them. The vast majority looked like sweet-potato mounds of earth with sticks on top fixed to resemble a cross. I walked over these unmarked graves looking for my brother's, a hard task as they all looked the same to me. In the distance were small clusters of people huddled around a freshly dug grave. Some were holding funerals, their sorrowful songs identifying them as Catholic, Methodist, Salvationist, Anglican, etc.

I found Robert's grave at last. Weeds were growing all over it and I pulled out what I could, though the hard dry earth meant that I often left the roots intact. I laid my flowers on the grave, then remembered I had to break the stalks otherwise they would just be stolen and re-sold. Grave robbers worked shifts here too. A funeral had been turned into an exercise to prevent theft. On the day of the burial, before we had lowered him down, men stepped forward to bash the coffin and scar it so it would be of no value for anyone who might be thinking of digging it up and selling it. Despite that there was a risk his suit would be stolen. It was a hopeless battle, as the cemetery had no guards.

I knelt down and couldn't believe that my brother was lying under this dry mound. It wasn't so long ago that we had seen him off at the airport. He wore a black suit, white shirt and the flowery tie that I had bought for him when he got his teaching job. We all shed tears and he promised to be back soon. After all, he only wanted to work in England until he had enough money to buy a house and then he would return. He sent the family money and also worked hard to buy his own home. There was always something more to be done or someone else to educate; so, in the end, he felt he had to stay in the UK to support the family. Then his visa expired and he couldn't return, not even for a holiday.

There was a time when he would call me to say that he was on a bus returning from a night shift at one nursing home and going to a morning shift at another. It seems his whole life revolved around work. He had hoped to get into teaching but without the right visa it was just not possible. In any case they didn't need English teachers in England. He wrote about how stupid the people there could be. I never imagined white people could be stupid. He met people who had never read Shakespeare and couldn't form a proper sentence in their own native tongue – though in this respect it looked as if my own daughter might be taking the same route.

We kept wondering when he would tell us that he had got himself a white wife, and a little coloured nephew for me. The last call I ever got from that Godforsaken place was from a policeman telling us that he was dead. They had found my number on his mobile. He had bought his first car and was driving from work when he fell asleep behind the wheel.

"Bhudi Robbie is dead," I cried and dropped the phone.

"That can't be true," Baba had said, rising from his chair.

Mother fainted, and the whole house was shrouded in grief.

It cost five thousand pounds to repatriate his body. This was a sum we could not afford but Robert was organised, to the very last. He had life insurance and there was money to bring him home and to pay for his funeral. I was glad because I'd heard many stories about Zimbabweans who'd died in the Diaspora whose bodies could not be sent home. There were families who never found the closure that comes from seeing your loved one committed to the ground.

However, the unity that we felt when our collective tears soaked the earth was destroyed by what happened afterwards. The house in Eastlea, that Robert had saved up for for so long, had just been purchased and the title deeds signed. One thing about a people who have seen death as often as we have is the fact that everyone knows the question that will prey on people's minds even before the body grows cold.

WHO IS GOING TO GET WHAT?

We become carnivores circling each other. But, once again, Robert had thought of everything. He was only twenty-five but it seems as though he knew he was running on borrowed time. He'd left a will and a lawyer arranged by the British Embassy came round and read it to us.

He was a mouse-like man with whiskers who sweated beneath his heavy winter suit. I soon formed a low opinion of him. What kind of lawyer drives a Mazda 323?

Everyone else fell over themselves to try and please him, as if that would change the contents of the will he was holding before him on thick white paper. He was sitting in Baba's chair, the best in the house, though the springs must have poked his backside or else he had haemorrhoids because he kept shifting about as if he was trying to scratch his bottom.

Once we were all gathered he began, and I was not too impressed by his English. He had a thick Shona accent with r's where his l's should have been.

"Thank you for werucoming me in the house. As you aru know,

your son reft a wiri which we were given by the Bhuritish Embassy…" he went on to read and explain a number of legal issues before getting down to brass tacks. The house was so quiet you could hear a pin drop. His clothes, which were to be shipped over in due course, were to be shared among all the male relatives gathered. An uncle and aunt got his TV set, which he must never have watched when he was alive. As the list of his worldly possessions was read out, I felt it was a deconstruction of what his life had been in England, sterile and functional.

The part everyone was waiting for was about the house. I had overheard Takesure and Knowledge, our two eldest brothers, discussing it in the weeks before. Takesure, being the oldest, would take the main house and Knowledge and his wife could live in the cottage.

"I give my entire interest in the property, which I have purchased in full together with any insurance on such real property, but subject to any encumbrances on the said real property to my sister Vimbai Hozo and my niece Chiwoniso Mabayo. If said devisee fai-rus or devisees fai-ru to survive me then this gift sharu lapse and become part of the residue of my estate."

I shook my head unable to believe what I was hearing. If I hadn't been supported I would have swooned on the spot. Takesure leapt up and grabbed the will from the lawyer's hands.

"What's the meaning of this?" He tore it in half and threw it on the floor.

The lawyer shrunk back in the chair but Takesure grabbed him by the collar and shook him so hard that his head bobbled like some sort of rag doll.

"Porice, Porice!" the poor lawyer shouted. He was given a hard slap across the face.

"Let him go. It doesn't change anything," Baba said, prising the lawyer from Takesure's furious grip. The lawyer shot off like a bolt shouting that he would sue. He didn't sue, and remained the executor of the estate to the very end.

The following months were full of wrangling. Takesure and Knowledge threatened to beat me up if I didn't sign the house over to them. It was as though they felt entitled to it by rights. Baba and Mother agreed that the house should go to them. 'What if I got married?' they argued. The family would lose the house. I would have given in, if half of that inheritance didn't belong to Chiwoniso. I had to protect her birthright.

Takesure and Knowledge moved their families forcibly into the house. It was only after months of going to and fro to the courts that they were evicted by the police. I endured endless threats, which only stopped when I won a peace order barring my family from being a hundred metres near me or my house.

€ight

I got to the salon early and on time on Monday morning. I have a sixth sense about things and felt that on the one weekend I'd been away something radical had happened. The smirk on Agnes' face as she greeted me confirmed my fears. She had just opened shop and was arranging the stocks.

"Mama wants to see you later."

"What about?"

"I don't know. Your habitual lateness I suppose."

"Everyone knows what time I come in." My threat about how I brought in half the customers lingered on my tongue. I wouldn't waste it on Agnes, she was too stupid "So how did Dumisani do on his first day?" I tried to sound as disinterested as I could with my question.

Agnes put the packs of hair products she was holding down and faced me. There was a glint in her eye. Some sort of devilish aura emanated from her.

"That's for you to find out later," she said and waited for me to speak. It was clear she wanted me to grovel. I went to the kettle instead and boiled some water.

Dumisani, Yolanda and Memory came in together. They were laughing at something as if they were all old friends.

"There is the wonder boy himself," Agnes said, giving Dumisani a hug. She might have suffocated him in those folds of fat if he had not pulled back to catch his breath.

"You must be Vimbai," he said, coming over and kissing me on both cheeks. I was unused to this type of greeting and found it wholly inappropriate.

"I am looking forward to seeing you work," I said coldly.

"That can't be true. I have heard about your work. I honestly can't wait to see you at it. There is so much I can learn from you." He laughed and I felt disarmed.

"Dumi is lying. He knows his work is much better than yours." The words sunk in as Agnes studied my face trying to see if she had achieved the desired effect. My brows knitted against my will.

"That's not the case," Dumi said, smiling a little.

I looked at Yolanda and Memory and their faces dropped to the floor. I reminded myself I was the Queen Bee here and poured myself a cup of tea. I arranged my chair and got ready for the first customer.

She came in soon after. A professional-looking lady with tons of make up on. She was not a regular so I pointed her to my chair. Mrs Khumalo insisted that I styled new customers myself to guarantee they came back.

"I am looking for a guy called Dumi to do my hair," she said as she sat down.

"It's okay, I'll do it," I replied.

"I want Dumi, he did my cousin's hair on Saturday and she told me that he's really good."

The other girls exchanged conspiratorial glances, which I felt behind my back. Dumi moved in to save me further embarrassment.

"Don't worry, Vimbai. It will give you a chance to finish your tea," he turned to the woman and asked, "Who's your sister?"

"Her name is Mercy, you must remember her. She's very light-skinned like a coloured girl."

"I remember now," said Dumi with his trademark chortle.

"I want you to give me the same style as her."

"No."

"What do you mean 'no'?" the lady said half-rising from the seat just as Mrs Khumalo came in.

"She's a customer. Give her what she wants." I rather wanted Mrs Khumalo to hear me say that.

"I'll take my money someplace else."

"What's the problem?" Mrs Khumalo asked.

"She wants me to give her her sister's hair style but I can make her look better than that."

The customer stopped in her tracks. That's the power of vanity, the desire to go one up. "What are you proposing?"

"I want to cut your hair short."

Instinctively the woman reached for her shoulder-length hair. It was well looked after; her crowning glory. I expected her to bolt, but she seemed rooted to the spot like a rabbit caught in the headlights as Dumi drew nearer. He took her hand and drew closer.

"You have beautiful eyes and your long hair tilts the balance away from your fine face. Your cheeks are sculpted but your long hair makes it impossible to admire them. Trust me."

There was magnetism about him that lured her in. She sat back silently in the chair. I could see her shaking slightly as if she was unsure of herself. Dumi took a large towel and covered the mirror so she could not see her reflection in it.

"Trust me," he said gently. We were all watching the scene trying to make sense of it.

He picked up a large pair of scissors and in one quick movement took a snip from the hair on the left side of her head. The woman shuddered as the hairs floated down to the ceramic floor, landing on both the black and white squares. If the mirror had been uncovered she would certainly have fled. He began to snip furiously and the hair grew into a small pile at his feet.

"Come outside. We've got to talk," Mrs Khumalo said to me.

I went out with her and she drew me toward the lawn out of earshot. Two half-naked toddlers, her late brother's children, were playing beneath the clothes line in the yard.

"Is everything okay?" I asked.

"We have to talk about your attendance. I have reports that you come in late every day and stand around whilst customers are waiting. I will not allow this sort of behaviour. I hope you understand me. Consider this your final warning."

She walked away from me without waiting for a reply. I wanted to say something but my throat had a lump in it. I wanted to tell her that most of the customers in her shop wanted me and I could go at any time leaving her without any customers but I could not. To be dispensable is a woman's worst nightmare and I was beginning to live it.

Everything was a blur for me back in the salon. I stared at the half drunk cup of tea on the table, which I could no longer stomach. Dumi worked with a furious passion. He seemed in a trance as he put the final touches to the lady's hair. She slouched in her chair, her eyes closed as he worked his magic. There was fluidity to his movements that I had never seen before. Finally he was finished. He crouched in front of her and asked:

"Are you ready to see the new you?"

He uncovered the mirror with a flourish and stood beside it with his head slightly bowed. The lady stood up and walked closer to the mirror. She touched her face as if to check if the person in the mirror was really her. I could see a glint in her eye, a slight quiver of her lower lip.

We all held our breath desperate for her verdict. She swallowed hard. Dumi stepped behind her and peered into the mirror over her shoulder.

"I look like Halle Berry." She sounded breathless. Her voice was a tiny whisper.

"There are some women like Halle Berry or Toni Braxton whose beauty is beyond ordinary. A face such as yours is a rare thing and it must be shown to the whole world." He adjusted a spike in her hair to make sure it was perfect.

The girls broke out in spontaneous applause. I had never seen anything like it before in this salon or any other. Dumi had a boyish grin on his face. The woman began to thank him profusely but he thanked her in return for allowing him to work on her. I felt my palms grow sweaty and my chest tighten. It was a feeling I was unused to. Then I couldn't have named it, but later I realised that this was jealousy.

Mrs Khumalo had a proud motherly smile on her face as she accepted payment from the lady. She went as far as to claim that she had trained Dumisani herself. I recalled a time when she hung over my clients and bragged about my abilities. I tried to comfort myself by telling myself that my styles were better but when I looked at the supermodel who was about to leave our salon self-doubt crept in.

"I work at Deloitte and Touche as a chartered accountant. I am sure the other girls will want to know where I got my hair done. I will be sure to tell them about this young man."

True to her word, that afternoon, the phone rang off the hook with accountants, receptionists and secretaries from her firm looking for appointments.

Nine

A new spot on my face was bothering me. It was deep in my chin and nothing I could do seemed to get rid of it. It was there on display for the whole world to see. It was only a fortnight since Dumi had started and the salon was twice as busy. We stopped allowing people to come in without appointments except for the barber side of things where business had only mildly improved. The books were full and we worked longer hours. It was hard to do your styling when every five minutes the phone was ringing with yet another request for an appointment.

The star of the show was Dumi of course. The ladies said his name with a phoney accent. Whenever he nipped out there were comments on how cute he was, how great his body was. "To find a man who can groom himself in Zimbabwe is next to impossible, but what are the odds of finding one who can groom you as well?" someone said. He would chat with the girls and feel like one of them. A man so comfortable with his own masculinity was hard to find.

Until now no one had bothered to find out how he had become a hairdresser or where he had learnt his trade. They all took it for granted that he had always been this hair god. He also started something, which we had heard of but never thought to have in our salon. I can recall my horror when he asked one client (we no longer called them customers) what contraception she was using.

Charlie Boy looked mortified and pretended to read a newspaper, which was a week old.

"My boyfriend and I use condoms," the woman said not offended in the least bit.

"All the time?"

"Of course."

"That's really good. You have to look after yourself with all the stuff going about. Have you heard about the femidom?" he said, taking a pack out of his bag, which was on the floor.

"I've heard of the female ones but I've never seen one."

He pulled one out of its package and dangled the 'femidom'. It was a wide rubber sheath with a large ring one side and a smaller closed ring at the other end. He looked like a high school teacher and no one felt the least embarrassed. His slender fingers stretched it out for all of us to see.

"It is very simple to use. You have to put it on before there is any contact between the umm, squeeze the small ring here like this and put it in your umm umm, the outer ring goes over your opening to protect the sides from any nasties and then the thing goes in there and you're in business. It's just that simple and there are instructions on the pack."

The lady actually held it and played around with it. It was passed round for all our customers to see.

"Are you sure it won't get swallowed?"

"It is better than the condoms and less likely to slip."

"Do you have any more of these?"

"I have some samples if anyone wants to try them out. We'll be getting a shipment next week and after that they go on sale. They're very cheap too."

"I like this. It gives me control because sometimes men don't like to strap on." Everyone took one from him including Charlie Boy who claimed it was for an 'experiment'. Agnes hid hers in a paper bag with knitwear. I refused, saying I didn't sleep around so I didn't need one. The truth is I couldn't bear taking anything from him. I was wondering what Mrs Khumalo would do when she realised that her place of business was being turned into a brothel. I didn't have to wait long for an answer.

Mrs Khumalo walked in and there was a rush to hide the incriminating devices. The only person who didn't make it on time was Dumi who was holding the rubber sheath high above his head. The whole room went silent.

"Vimbai, can you tell me what's going on in here?" she said

"Ask Dumisani." I was quick to deflect the heat off myself.

She stood arms akimbo waiting for her explanation. I was so sure the charmer in Dumi did not stand a chance against the Catholic in Mrs Khumalo.

"I'm showing the ladies some femidoms. I got them from an NGO and we can sell them here in the shop."

"You should put some posters up so that our clients know we're selling them. I don't know why no one else has thought of doing this. Very soon all the salons will be copying us, just you wait and see." I scratched my ears, unsure if I was hearing right. Everyone in the place giggled like one nervous choir. We didn't know that for a woman like Mrs Khumalo, it was a simple calculation. Make a little extra on the condoms and if her customers lived longer, then they could keep coming in and putting money in her till.

The golden boy could do no wrong.

***

There were two brown envelopes on the table when I got home. I knew exactly what they were. Chiwoniso tugged my sleeve.

"Mummy is busy. Go and play with Sisi Maidei."

She tugged my sleeve again with more vigour. My hand moved of its own accord. The next thing I remember was my child, on the floor, bawling. Maidei came rushing in and picked her up. She held Chiwoniso close to her chest. I waved her away with my hand. It was the first time I'd ever laid my hands on my baby. Her subdued cries tore my heart apart.

The city council wanted its rates paid and ZESA had sent me a final notice before my electricity supply would be cut off. If it had not been for the cash Robert had left me I would not have made it this far. That was spent and it would take my entire salary to keep this place without leaving anything for Chiwoniso's school fees. Why was her father being such an idiot?

I love my daughter but there are times when I look at her face and become angry seeing just how much of her father is in it. When I became pregnant, he changed like a light that's been flicked off.

"You weren't even a virgin when I first fucked you. How do I know it's mine?" He knew very well why I wasn't a virgin and to use this in such a callous way really cut me. There's a proverb that tells how tender men are when they're courting but once they get what they want they change entirely. I hadn't expected this of Phillip: he was different. He said he loved me; he said he would leave his wife for me. I was too young to know that there was nothing new in such lies.

It wasn't long before I heard rumours of how there were half a dozen or so girls dotted around the country in the exact same predicament. For the first few months of Chiwoniso's life, Phillip was absent. Then one day he sent a driver to my home with some money and nappies. He even called later that day to find out how the baby was. It gave me the slightest glimmer of hope but it was foolish hope.

I didn't see him at all for the next five years, but I was grateful for the envelopes of money when they came. It paid for my daughter's school, clothing, food, medicine, and then one day he showed up at my gate. It was just after I'd moved to Eastlea. He staggered out of the car holding a beer bottle, the contents of which were spilling everywhere.

"I want to see my daughter," his words slurred.

"Phillip, what's wrong with you? She's asleep, come back tomorrow," I said, irritated.

He pinned me to the door and tried to kiss me. I said no and told him that he was drunk. "I don't care you bitch. I pay you my money every month so that you can live in a nice house and wear fine clothes. You are my bitch and I can have you any time I want." He tried again but he was so drunk, I overpowered him and pushed him out of the house. He shouted obscenities and smashed the living room window before he drove off in a drunken stupor.

The payments stopped soon after that. There were people who told me to take him to court and get a maintenance order, but I was too proud. I would not give him an excuse to try to gain access to my daughter. As she grows older, I know she will begin to ask questions about her father but that is a bridge I will cross later. Till then, keeping her safe is my priority. Now, I needed more money.

Ten

The music in the salon changed to Urban Grooves, a local bastardized form of hip hop with no artistic merit. When Dumi first brought it in, I thought it was a one-off. Soon the imitation synthesised beats were playing every day. Nobody seemed to mind except me. The artists with names like Maskiri, Willom Tight, Rocqui, Extra Large, singers who I'd paid no attention to in the past, now dominated the salon's airwaves. The music was like listening to pans smashed together by a three-year-old.

"This music has no lyrical content at all."

"You're not listening to them. They are talking about love, hustling for money in these tough times, unity, small houses, everyday life, and with themes that are relevant to the youths of today." Dumi stepped up to defend his music.

"You can't even hear what they're saying underneath those phoney American accents."

"You can't hear what those Rhumba artists you love are saying either."

"At least their music is part of our culture."

"Correct me if I am wrong but I believe you're saying that artists from the DRC are expressing our culture, but kids who grew up in these streets are not. I find that absurd to say the least." He pursed his lips in a way I found disgusting.

He couldn't understand that Rhumba music is universal and crosses the barriers of language, space and time. When Awilo Longomba sings about love you feel it, when he is sad you become sad with him. Now I had to endure the damn Urban Grooves that made my head ache.

Still, today was at least the first Tuesday of the month and Trina was coming. We all looked forward to her monthly visits.

It was not long before the rumble of her diesel pick-up could be heard from the street. That car sounded more like a grinding mill than a form of transport. She pulled in and parked just in front of the doors. Her tall white frame stepped out of the car. She was wearing sunglasses – in fact I had never seen her without a pair. The khaki trousers and shirt she wore underlined her lack of dress sense for someone who was only in her early thirties.

"*Makadini madzimai,*" she greeted us with a full Zezuru accent.

"*Tiripo makadini,*" we all replied like a primary school choir. There was never a time when we spoke to her in English. For all we knew she might not have been able to speak the language. The freckles on her face said she was one of us and had been basking in the glory of the same sun for far too long.

"Is Mrs Khumalo in? She made a big order and I have to make sure I've got everything right."

"You've just missed her but I know what she ordered," Agnes said stepping outside.

They returned with two full boxes of hair-care products.

"There was also the human hair if you brought it."

"I couldn't get any but I have some synthetic instead if you want it," Trina said, shrugging her shoulders.

"It will have to do then," replied Agnes, as Trina returned for another boxful.

The two of them counted the stock and verified that it was correct. It was reassuring to know that we had supplies for the coming month. Mostly it was Dark and Lovely together with Revlon because we could source the low-quality stuff locally.

Agnes went back inside the house and returned with six two-litre bottles of cooking oil. She continued back and forth until she had loaded twenty-four of them into the truck. Trina rarely took money when she could help it. Further down the line she would trade the cooking oil for something else, petrol perhaps or even bales of toilet paper. Anything was better than carrying around large stacks of notes.

She had once been in farming. Together with her husband, they had owned two farms: one in Beatrice, which she had inherited from her father, and another just outside the city along Chinhoyi Road, which belonged to her husband, Derek Price. When the land reform programme began, they were quick to give up the farm in Beatrice in the hope they would be allowed to keep Good Hope farm on which they grew tobacco and other cash crops.

This gesture had seen them through the first wave of invasions and they had even received a letter from the government telling them they would be allowed to stay. It was almost a miracle as they had seen their neighbours picked off one by one. Then, just a year ago, a powerful minister had taken a liking to their green oasis that was now surrounded by vast deteriorating farms. They had been to court and won an injunction preventing the seizure of their farm.

But then the war vets arrived. Their workers were beaten, livestock slaughtered and their home ransacked. They fled and could not return. This government minister it was rumoured already had eight farms, which everyone knew about, and still wanted more.

When Trina spoke you could hear the echo of a plea. A sort of longing to be away from the bustle of the city, which must have been a culture shock for a girl who had grown up in wide open spaces. There was a kind of deliberateness in her gestures and a weariness to the way she carried herself. Perhaps she'd hoped that one day they would win their farm back. If she did, she never said a thing to us. They'd bought a house in Harare and now her husband made a living selling cars that they had shipped in from overseas. When she went with him to the port in Durban, she bought supplies for businesses around the city and had become something of a legend.

Her success came from keeping her word, something we could

never hope for from any of our other suppliers.

"I brought some presents for you girls," she said peering into her car and coming out with some brightly coloured packets that we strained to make out from afar. She toyed with us for a bit trying to make us guess what they were. You can't believe how we all shrieked with joy when she finally revealed that they were packs of tampons. I had been using cotton balls for four months – it was as bad as that – and I considered myself lucky to have them. There were no pads in the shops. We had all scoured the city. I knew of other women using rags that they would then wash and reuse and shuddered at the prospect that one day I might be compelled to follow suit. She had one packet left in her hand when she asked, "Where's Patricia?"

"She was fired."

"Oh" she said cupping her mouth.

"I'm her replacement but somehow I don't think those will do me any good." Dumi promptly introduced himself. Before she had a chance to speak he went over and touched her hair. "You're a mess."

Trina went over to the mirror and ran her hand through her hair.

"It's not so bad."

"Look at it. This just won't do. Sit in this chair." He literally forced her into the chair.

"I don't mean to be rude but have you ever worked with hair like mine?" she protested, trying to squirm out as he held her down.

"Madam, even if you were a baboon, I would still style you. I work with all types of hair."

He shampooed and conditioned her, untangling her frizzy hair. He ran a comb through and tried to style her before he decided that she would do well with simply tying it back in a ponytail, "We need to straighten it, and I can imagine putting a few blonde highlights in it. Pity we don't have the dye or the straighteners to work with. If you can get me the materials I need, I guarantee that I will make you look so hot your husband will not recognise you."

"God it's been ages since I've been in a salon. Tell me what you need and maybe next month I'll come round with some products and you can style me."

Dumi wrote down a list of what he wanted her to bring along for the next visit. He was adamant that it would be on the house since she was our supplier. We watched her walking back to the car, her usual step replaced by swaying hips. It was the most feminine I'd ever seen her.

She drove off and I stashed my tampons in my handbag. If I could have willed my period on I would have, knowing that I had these. At that time though, none of us could have known that Dumi's little stunt was going to have some devastating ramifications for the salon and our relations with Trina.

Eleven

Work was becoming an ordeal, I felt physically ill each time I made my way into the salon. To endure the mind-numbing thumping beats of the music they all now seemed to prefer was torture in itself. The salon was busier; in fact we had more clients on the books than we could cope with. Dumi wasn't content. He tore down the old posters that we had on the walls and replaced them with glossy ones that he said had come from America. The ones opposite my chair showed skimpy women with intricate braids who I was forced to look at every day. Others were brightly coloured, advertising various hairstyles that I'd never seen before.

The posters that really got to me were ones with a smiling man and a woman staring into each other's eyes. Below that was a pack of femidoms tied with a red ribbon. We were a salon and not a brothel, for Christ's sake. Not only did we have to take money for the hair we did, but Mrs Khumalo now insisted that we push the condoms onto each woman who sat on our chairs. I'd never felt more like a slut in my entire life. I thought briefly of leaving and getting a job somewhere else. Where would I go, who would employ me? The thought left my mind as soon as it popped in.

"It looks like there is something on your mind. You don't quite seem yourself today." Lucy was one of my regulars. I was grateful that she had not joined the mindless minions who insisted that only Dumisani could do their hair.

"Times are hard my sister."

"It's the same for all of us. Hard times never kill."

It was easy for her to say that with her perfect husband and family.

I was plaiting cornrows. It was an intricate style that I was giving her, with the lines curving in wavy motions round her head.

"Ahh that's too tight.'

"Sorry, I will make them a little looser."

"She must be thinking about a man." Agnes commented with a simper.

"Why don't you just shut up?" I retorted.

"Someone's in a bad mood today. So it can only be a man!" Dumi joked her a wink. In a way he was right, it was a man – him. "You know we're just teasing you Vimbai," he tried to placate me.

I wasn't in a forgiving mood and ignored him, concentrating on the scalp in front of me I had to will my fingers to move in the way I wanted them to, conciously focusing on what I was doing, whereas before Dumi'd arrived, they'd moved as naturally as walking. Also, now, I noticed flaws in my work that I hadn't seen before. One line of the cornrows was thicker than the others. I undid it quietly and redid it. Lucy fidgeted. I knew she was thinking the braids were too tight, but this was the way I'd always done them. That it had become a problem made me feel awful. Had I been getting this wrong for years?

Lucy flinched and said, "I forgot to tell you all something… Abbas and Sons is getting a delivery of sugar tomorrow."

"Is that the shop that's down town?"

"It's on Rezende."

"Can you organise some for us?"

"My brother works for them and I'll be there tomorrow morning. You should send someone to meet me first thing in the morning."

"We will send…"

"One of you will have to come because it has to be someone that I know." Of all the reasons for continuing to work at the salon, this had to be the best one. It was the centre of a network where you could hear about what stuff was going on, which was essential when so much was in short supply. Maize meal, sugar, salt and cooking oil were the basics that one always had to be on the look out for, especially when you could get them at the gazetted price and sell them on the black market for a quick profit. I volunteered to meet up with Lucy.

The next morning I left home early making sure Maidei warmed some water for Chiwoniso's bath. I had had to switch off the geyser to save on electricity. It would have to be that way until things improved. I got a lift from a man who was pirating and he dropped me off at the main post office. It took me time to cross the street because the traffic light was not working and no one wanted to give way. Cars, or rather their drivers, pushed and hooted madly trying to cross Jason Moyo Avenue. Heroically I ran and weaved my way across the mayhem, knowing that pedestrians would always get short shrift. It was not a feat for the faint-hearted. I stopped to catch my breath leaning on the metal railings that fenced Town House. The old building stood in its glory as if the colonial times were mocking the failure of our independent era. It was still the City Council headquarters. The colourful Zimbabwean flag drooped impotently in the smog-filled stagnant atmosphere.

There was a curious feature in the square in front of the building. It was a silverish metallic ball with spikes that looked like a hastily cobbled piece of modern art by a D grade O-level student. It was the fountain, from which not a drop of water ran. If my memory serves me right it cost nearly a million when it was built, quite a fortune then, though it wouldn't buy a loaf of bread now. When it worked it produced a curious ball of water that was outstandingly unspectacular. It was quick to break down, just months after it was unveiled. Everything about the city council was broken except the official Mercs that made their way in and out of the gates, as if any real important business was taking place within.

It surprised me how with only ten per cent of the population employed, the streets were full of people bumping past each other first thing in the morning. I passed a vendor whose business consisted of selling single mints and single sticks of cigarette as I turned into Robert Mugabe Road. From there it was just a couple more steps onto Rezende Street.

Abbas and Sons was a largish Indian store, one of several in the down-town area. There was a queue of about sixty people already there. A hand grabbed me from behind. I quickly turned clutching my handbag.

"It's only me," Lucy said. She was wearing a *dhuku*, headkerchief, over her hair as if embarrassed by the hairstyle I'd given her less than twenty-four hours previously. I pretended not to notice. "Give me the money." She took the brick-like bundle of cash I had and stuffed it into her own large handbag. She did not need to count it. We can tell the value of money from its weight. It wouldn't even matter if it was a few hundred thousand short anyway, the way its value was falling by the hour.

"Good morning," I said to her.

"Let's go round to the back," she whispered and turned. We stepped past piles of rubbish and avoided puddles of brown water as we went up the back street. Lucy kept looking around worried that someone might follow us. There was something exciting about doing this. She dialled her cellphone, whispered a few brisk words and hung up.

"Just wait, he will be out soon."

Soon was an hour and a quarter later. The door opened suddenly and a scrawny man with a shiny face stepped out.

"Chop-chop," he said thrusting a bag at her and taking the money in one swift motion. My heart pounded as if I was taking part in a drug deal. As soon as he was done the man went back in and shut the door. That was it. We had our sugar. Lucy gave me three two-kilogram packets of white and one two-kilogram packet of brown and we parted ways. She had just earned herself a free session the next time she came into the salon. Once I got back to the salon, we would break the packets into smaller packs of about a kilogram each because we had a few more shareholders in this operation, clients who had been in when Lucy made her announcement.

I walked back onto the street. The queue was twice as long now and snaking its way on to Robert Mugabe. People were shoving and pushing each other. A group of policemen appeared at the front with batons and took control, making sure everyone kept their place in the queue. The truth is by giving up their time to baton a few people they'd earned themselves a place at the head of the queue. I made my way up the road smiling and feeling like an angel. If I didn't have four kilograms on either side I would have floated away high above the skyscrapers.

Twelve

To see Fungai standing at the gate and waiting for me to unlock it was a dream come true. For an instant I could almost believe that one day I would host my family here, in peace. It was his first time coming. He had ignored the Takesure/Knowledge saga. I let him in and gave him a big hug.

"I thought you were just blowing hot air when you said you would visit."

"I'm not sure if 'blowing hot air' is the right metaphor. Anyway, I always try to do what I say."

He was panting and I held his hand fearful that he might turn around and walk away.

"You're squeezing my hand too hard," he laughed. When I let go he put his arm around me. I felt like he was leaning on me because I could feel his weight on my shoulder. "It's a beautiful house. Robert did well."

Now it was my turn to squeeze his hand, glad that he had invoked our deceased brother. There were times when I missed him in this big house, but being with Fungai was good because his face reminded me of Robert. They were just a year apart and seeing Fungai I could almost picture how our older brother might have looked today.

"Do you mind if we sit down for a minute."

"But I want to show you the house."

"We can do it later. My feet are killing me."

"Let me guess… you walked all the way here. Some things never change"

Fungai had a weird theory that he should walk everywhere. There was no way of discouraging him when he made his mind up on something. He claimed that as a 'philosopher' walking brought him closer to the 'truth'. When pressed on the matter he would claim that there was a natural state for all things to be in. Cars were unnatural and because they moved unnaturally fast, one couldn't see the world for what it really was. When walking one was closer to the world and observed it more closely. I didn't agree with this romantic theory, which meant that he would never find himself outside of the city unless… it was too crazy to even contemplate.

We sat down under the shade of a musasa tree in the garden. A soft wind wafted the sweet scent of its green flowers toward us. The swaying leaves made a gentle rustling sound. Maidei came out with a glass of water and greeted him. He drank it in one gulp and asked for another.

"So you have a maid now. You look like a little madam sitting there having everything done for you." I prayed that he would not launch a tirade about the evils of capitalism and exploitation.

"I'm glad you've come, even if you are going to tease me!"

"I would have come sooner but I have been busy at the university."

"They let you back in?"

"No, with them it's all about money. Some lecturers allow me to sit in during their classes. The librarian is a friend and he lets me in though he doesn't allow me to borrow books. I make a bit of money writing essays for students who can't do them themselves."

"One day we'll have enough money for you to finish your course."

"Pah, I don't want to," a bitter smile flashed across his face for a split second. "All that matters is accumulating knowledge. I'm thankful I can still do that at least."

"You applied for that scholarship at Fort Hare. Maybe it will come through."

"Everyone knows they only give those to people with connections."

We were silent for a while. He was right. A lot of things depended on who you knew and our family was as unconnected as you could get. Maidei returned and gave him some more water. I thought he might be hungry so I asked her to cook dinner right away.

"We're almost out of firewood," she said as she left.

"I will take care of it.'

"It's funny how we seem trapped between modernity and the past. We have power lines yet half the time no electricity runs through them. We have cars, but no petrol to run them on, mobiles but the network is intermittent." He picked up a blade of dry grass and played around with it. I loved to listen to him. He always sounded so intelligent. In a fairer world he would have become someone important, a teacher maybe.

"How's the rest of the family?"

"They're fine. Nothing has changed "

"How did the memorial go?" I asked. It was a roundabout way to ask what the family was saying about me, and Fungai knew it.

"It went well, all things considered. Uncle Mhandu managed to get a nice tombstone for Robert – black granite with gold lettering. Maybe one day you and I can go and see it together."

"There's no way I'm walking all the way to Mbudzi with you."

He laughed. "They're still as divided as ever about this whole issue. I asked them if a house was worth losing a daughter and a grandchild over. And I get the feeling that they know they're wrong, but they can't say it. In our culture a parent does not apologise to their child. You know that already. But there is something you could do to smooth things over."

"Like what?"

"Apologise."

"Like hell I will. I am not the one in the wrong here. I made an effort to see them at the memorial and they turned me away like a dog. As far as I'm concerned that was the last straw. You're my only family now."

"Don't say things like that. Blood is sacred."

"Says you, the one who doesn't even believe in God."

"Just because I don't believe in a Judaeo-Christian white vengeful deity does not mean that I have no conception of right and wrong. Doesn't the Bible say, 'Honour your father and your mother, that your days may be long in the land that the Lord your God is giving you.' Exodus 20 verse 12. 'Children, obey your parents in the Lord, for this is right.' Ephesians 6 verse 1. I could go on you know."

"That's not what I'm trying to say."

"The point is whether they were wrong or not in this, they're your parents and you must make peace with them. It's you who has to make a move."

"What of Takesure and Knowledge?"

"I don't care about them. They're your siblings. They're young and have long to live. It is *baba na amai* that are important."

"I am not ready yet."

"Swallow your pride."

Chiwoniso came running and leapt onto his lap. "Uncle Fungai, what have you brought for me?" He hugged her and laughed.

"Greet your uncle properly." I told her.

"Oh come on, leave my niece alone."

"She has to learn to do it the right way otherwise one day she will embarrass me."

She clapped her hands and said, '*Makadini* Sekuru Fungai.' He smiled and replied, '*Ndiripo wakadini hako muzukuru.*' He gave her a bar of chocolate, which she opened and ate right away. If only I had had loving uncles in my day.

She was still in her blue and white school uniform so I sent her away to change. I was angry that Maidei had let her go off to play in her uniform. It was expensive and I couldn't afford to get her another one if something happened to it before the year was out. The sound of her tiny voice singing as she went to the house calmed me.

"I can't believe she still remembered me."

"She's a clever girl."

"Like her mother."

"I think she takes after her uncle there." We laughed and reminisced on the old days and gossiped about the new. When you are away from family for so long, it is amazing just how much you miss out on.

The tour of the main house was a success. In a way the spirit of Robert lingered as if he wanted us all here, together, as one family before he could finally move on. Fungai agreed with me and said that he felt it too. I offered him a room for the night. He told me that he fancied staying for a bit so that he could work on the garden and help out. The cottage had remained an anti-climax. The broken windows gave it a run-down appearance like something from a ghost town. Broken glass crunched under our feet as I showed him round.

"What happened here?"

"Mukoma Knowledge and his family."

"You mean they just vandalised the whole place and you didn't tell us?"

"I have never had a chance to. I will fix it up one day when I get the money."

"You could rent it out to a small professional family. This is losing you a lot in potential dollars."

Thirteen

The white Mercedes pulling up on the driveway reinforced my ego. Despite everything that had happened I still had the number one client. There were few people who got close to a government minister, let alone touched one. As she emerged from the car, my lips moved involuntarily of their own accord. She walked as gracefully as her weight would allow and Mrs Khumalo moved forward to greet her.

The minister was wearing a green African dress with a matching head wrap, both of which had pictures of Robert Mugabe imprinted on them like large polka dots. It was the design they had used during the last election campaign that had seen the party back into power. I shuddered when I remembered the youths in party T-shirts who terrorized Budiriro beating anyone who was suspected to be a member of the opposition. The minister entered and I gestured for her to sit in my chair.

"Not today, Vimbai. I want that young man to do it," the minister declared.

I thought I'd misheard her, so I said, "Beg your pardon."

"I've heard of this fine young man from my secretary. You know Mrs Ndoro? She comes here sometimes. Rumours are going around the city that you have competition Vimbai and so I wanted to see for myself."

"Only the very best for the minister," said Mrs Khumalo smugly.

My head was swooning. If I had not held on to one of the dryers I would have collapsed. This could not be happening. It felt like some sort of a nightmare, the one that comes like a daydream when your eyes are awake and you can't discern fact from fantasy.

Agnes was sniggering along with Yolanda. My knees felt wobbly so I crossed over to the cash desk, sat down and poured myself a glass of water. My entire career flashed before my very eyes.

"Come on Dumi, let's see you work your magic." Mrs Khumalo encouraged him because he was rooted to the spot looking my way as if checking out my reaction. There was a hint of pride in his face. I bit my tongue until I could taste the warm trickle of my own blood.

"Stand up, Vimbai. We have clients waiting."

Dumisani had convinced the minister to go for braids. They had bantered for a bit with her insisting she was too old for that sort of look, but Dumi prevailed. Mrs Khumalo frowned a bit because they took in excess of five hours to finish. For the chair to be tied up that long meant losing money.

As usual Dumi had a trick up his sleeve. He took the extensions and plaited them in just a quarter of the way and left the ends loose. His nimble fingers danced on top of her head for an hour until the last one was in place. I had never seen anyone work so fast with braids before. The minister looked at her face in the mirror and blinked arrogantly. It was the type of vanity a woman her age has when by sleight of hand she is made to look ten years younger.

"What do you think?" Dumi asked standing aside and admiring his handiwork.

"I think it looks lovely."

"It brings out your smile."

"You're trying to charm me. I am as old as your mother." She tried to leave the chair but he held her down.

"I am not finished yet. That's just the hair. Now let me give you style." With that he took the head wrap she'd worn and unbundled it. He grabbed a pair of scissors and cut it in half, right through Robert Mugabe's face. Mrs Khumalo tensed and held her breath. The one piece he folded in two lengthwise and placed over her head, tying it round the back. He cut through what remained of Mugabe in the other piece and rolled both of them. An almost imperceptible smirk lingered on the minister's face as Dumi did this. He tied the pieces of cloth around the minister's wrists as little bow ties.

"I don't know where you found this boy, Mrs Khumalo but this place will go far. I am going to tell the other ladies in the Women's League that this is the place to come. I am telling you – you will be swamped with customers."

We were already swamped with teachers, businesswomen, nurses, accountants, secretaries, bankers and now as if that wasn't enough we were going to be swamped with politicians. The way Mrs Khumalo looked at the walls said she was thinking of expanding the building once more.

The minister admired herself in the mirror, paid her dues and left beaming, her soul on cloud nine.

***

The day ended with Mrs Khumalo at the cash desk drinking a bottle of Fanta and arranging the bundles of money that were in a box. Yolanda and Memory were sweeping hair off the floor. I got my bag to leave when Dumi started to speak.

"How about a pay rise?" he said in his usual soft-spoken manner.

"Excuse me?" Mrs Khumalo replied putting her bottle down on the table with a bang.

"I said a pay increase would be nice." He was unfazed.

The girls who were sweeping stopped to watch. Even Charlie Boy strained to hear the exchange.

"You have been here less than three months and you already want a pay rise. I hope you remember you are still on your six month probationary period."

"I have been here three months and look what has happened. Your clientele has more than quadrupled. Revenues have gone up."

"I don't know where you are coming from but have you got any idea what it costs to run this salon? There are bills and rates to pay, not to mention the cost of the chemicals, which has gone up too," Mrs Khumalo retorted angrily. "You're so ungrateful. There are people out there who would bite your arm off to have your job for half the pay you are getting."

"Have you been on a kombi lately? The cost of living has gone up for us too and I think it is only fair that you give us a pay rise or else…"

"Or else what?" Mrs Khumalo raised one eyebrow.

Dumi shrugged his shoulders and headed for the door.

"Wait." She reached out for him. "Perhaps you're right. Let no one say the Khumalos are not fair employers. I want you to understand this is not because of any threat you can make. It is because I care about your welfare, all of you. I will give you a fifty per cent increment starting next month. How about that?"

"Inflation is too high. I say a hundred and fifty per cent with immediate effect."

Mrs Khumalo let out an involuntary groan like a woman stabbed in the back. "A hundred per cent, take it or leave it."

"With immediate effect?"

"Yes."

Dumi looked to the other girls who tried hard to contain their delight and then he looked at me. I was in turmoil, one half of me envious and the other delighted at what he had pulled off for us.

"We have a deal then. See you tomorrow morning."

The sun was setting as I walked through the jacaranda tree-lined streets from Baines Avenue to Leopold Takawira. Traffic was light today because petrol shortages were back. The few petrol stations that had any were rationing. I hoped I would be able to get transport all the same.

"Hey wait up," a voice called out to me.

I pretended not to hear and carried on. A set of footsteps pounded on the pavement and caught up with me.

"Hey Vimbai, didn't you hear me?" said Dumi panting.

"The traffic's too loud."

"I think you just thought I was a stalker. Listen I'm sorry about the whole thing with the minister today."

"Don't apologise, it's nothing at all. I'm kind of getting used to it."

My voice sounded gruff.

"I would never consciously try to take away your clients Vimbai."

"That's not what it looks like to me."

"At least let me try to make it up to you."

"How?"

He was silent. I began to walk away from him but he grabbed my shoulder. I stopped. He looked into my face and did that puppy thing with his eyes, which he pulled on clients in the salon. Stupid me!

I heard myself saying, "Great work with the pay rise thing. I need the cash."

"I need it badly too."

"What for if you don't mind me asking?"

"It's a long story, but let's say I was staying in Avondale with my Canadian friend, and now that he's left us, I can't afford the rent, so I need to move somewhere by next month."

Stupid me!

I did not like Dumi, or rather what Dumi was doing to me, making me feel second-best – me the best hairdresser in the salon – and yet I heard myself saying, "I was actually thinking of letting a room out at my place if you are interested."

Fourteen

It was not long before Dumisani moved in. I made him pay a modest deposit in the full knowledge that it would be eroded by inflation after the first month or two he was there. It all happened so quickly. I had never before expected a man to live in this house. The few days Fungai had stayed over, he left the toilet seat up and that was enough to drive me mad. What of this man, who was going to live with me for God-knows-how-long.

The day he moved in, I was surprised by just how much stuff he brought with him. For someone so young, he would hardly have had the time to accumulate all this gear. His TV had a 32-inch plasma screen so I moved my tiny Toshiba into my bedroom. He had a coffee table with a glass top and we put that in the lounge too. His radio was a massive Panasonic five CD changer. There were dozens of kitchen utensils all of which were superior to anything I had. The microwave was a welcome addition. I had never used one so Dumi taught me how to, reminding me never to put anything metallic in it. I banned Maidei from using it. It was too complicated for the stupid girl.

The sheer amount of clothes that he owned astounded me. His wardrobe was five times larger than mine with heaps of fashionable clothing that I had never seen in this city before. The toiletries that he put into the bathroom dominated the entire space. He had a dozen sweet-smelling perfumes, aftershave, imported bathing foams and shower gels. I hid my local stuff because it looked pitiful by comparison. He explained to me that the reason he had so much was that his Canadian friend had left a lot of things behind with him, because it was too expensive to send them back to his family.

"We're gonna have a blast living together," he gave a boyish grin.

The extra money that I was going to get from him would go some way in helping me with the bills and other things that I needed around the house. It was an unusual arrangement for a single woman to take in a male lodger, but I was freed from having to consider the feelings of my extended family. I could do what I liked and I didn't have to care for my reputation either, because I didn't want a man in my life. Ms Independent.

Dumi proved himself to be a considerate housemate. The toilet seat was left down. He washed the bath-tub after use and even helped Maidei with cleaning the house every so often. He was handy too. The first day he saw the cottage he went into action sweeping up all the broken glass. 'It might hurt the children,' he'd said. When that was done he got some clear plastic covers that Chiwoniso used for her exercise books and used them to cover the windows up. It was great having a handyman about when the light bulbs needed changing.

***

Catching the same kombi to and from work worked out for me as well. Seeing me with my handsome lodger, the perverts who used to make passes at me, all but stopped, except for the occasional cat whistle or crude remark.

Dumisani had piles of black magazines from abroad, which he told me were sent to him every couple of months by his cousin in America. I discovered his generous nature and he was happy for me to borrow any that I pleased. I plunged through piles of Black Beauty, Black Hair Styles and Care Guide, O, Pride, Hype Hair, Hair, Style and discovered that a lot of his work was taken from these publications. There were styles that were wholly original that he had come up with himself but I could see how having access to this wealth of information influenced his work.

He would ask me what I thought of a particular style and whether it could be done with the materials we had to work with. It was almost like all he ever thought about was the next huge style.

"What made you decide to go into hairdressing?" I asked him one day.

"I guess when I was at school I realised that I wanted to be a hairdresser."

"What school did you go to?"

"St. George's."

"Get out of here, a St George's schoolboy who becomes a hairdresser! That's the most ridiculous thing I've heard in my life."

"What's so ridiculous about it?"

"For starters, St George's kids come from loaded backgrounds. We're talking parents with serious amounts of cash."

"I had a rugby scholarship."

"A rugby scholarship! Since when have you been interested in sport? In any case don't all St George's students leave the country as soon as they're finished?"

"They can't all do that because I'm still here." He fished out his rugby jersey and waved it at me pointing at the number 15 sewn on. "I was captain too."

"I've got to say I'm kind of impressed but it must suck being the poor boy in a rich kids' school."

Dumi shrugged his shoulders.

"I guess that explains how you know about white people's hair because most of the kids there were white, when you were at school – right?"

"In a way it does. I started doing a friend's head and soon everyone was coming to me for haircuts and styling. I was a natural: black hair, white hair, it doesn't matter to me because something inside me just tells me how to do it. I've always excelled in everything I do in life, but I should stop bragging. Tell me how you got into hairdressing. I'm sure that would be a hell of a lot more interesting."

I told him how I'd learnt my craft in backyard salons in Budiriro, doing women's hair and experimenting there. I told him of my dream to open my own place one day and who knows, maybe some day own a string of top-end salons and boutiques. He listened to me with his head in his hands looking as if he was hanging on to every word I said.

***

That Saturday Dumi took Chiwoniso and me to Churchill Boys High School to watch some rugby. It would be the first game I'd ever watched in my life despite the fact that I lived so close to the school. We walked down the pine tree-lined Nigel Phillip Avenue. The school was massive with soccer fields on one side of the road and on the other hockey and rugby fields. Young boys in smart royal purple blazers and gray trousers doffed their caps and said, "Good afternoon sir – ma'am," as we passed by. It was amusing at first but by the time we reached the field my voice had grown hoarse from returning these greetings.

"It is even worse at St George's," Dumi said with a hint of pride.

The place was packed with parents and schoolchildren waiting for the main match. We found a place to sit at the pavilion and Dumi went off to get something to drink. A sound I had never heard before began to play. First there was a droning and then the roll of drums, then came a melody that was loud but sounded distinctly foreign. Chiwoniso clapped her hands to the beat.

"Look there's the Churchill Pipe Band. They're damn good." Dumi pointed at the group of school boys in skirts (kilts he called them) coming up the field followed by the rugby team in purple and white striped jerseys. They allowed their opponents on the pitch first. The spectators roared when the home side finally took to the field.

There was a hush and the Churchill boys performed a weird war cry of unintelligible words as they moved and performed an equally bizarre dance. Dumi explained that it was their ritual to perform the New Zealand 'Haka' before each game. But if their opponents were meant to be scared by the performance, they didn't look it at all.

"It's going to be a good game, they're playing Prince Edward who are equally as good," explained Dumisani watching the game with a keen pair of eyes. The ref blew his whistle and I felt Dumi's leg bouncing up and down as if he wished he was on the pitch himself.

The game progressed and he tried to explain the plethora of rules to me but I didn't understand them. All I could see were young boys

66

knocking each other on the head and fighting for a ball. It seemed so violent that I wondered why they even bothered having a referee on the pitch. The match ended with the home side narrowly victorious. Despite Dumi's passionate advocacy for the game, I told him that if this was what the sport was about then I had missed nothing in my life.

Fifteen

There was a changed atmosphere in the salon. Even Mrs Khumalo felt younger and oozed optimism. She began to talk about expanding the building for a third time. I can't tell you how worried we all were at that prospect. The roof would probably end up falling on our heads. I sat with Yolanda on the lawn for our lunch break. She was going to be off soon for her exams.

"I don't know how we will manage without you for three whole weeks."

"Three and a half actually."

A shadowy outline of a head showed briefly in the doorway. It was Dumisani's. Yolanda sighed.

"He's a damn fine brother," she said licking her forefinger and tapping her butt.

"I've seen better."

"Come on, he is living with you, so you can't honestly say that you haven't been tempted to do it."

"Don't be sick. He is like a little brother to me. How old is he anyway? Thirteen or something like that."

"Don't give me that; I have seen the way you look at him."

"More like the way you look at him. He is nearer your age anyway."

"No thanks, I've already got me a boyfriend."

"You sly thing, you. How come you didn't tell us?" I couldn't help squealing with delight. At least one of us had a boyfriend now.

"It's still far too early. It's only been a week you know." She had the look that was begging to be asked more.

"So what's he like?"

She went on to tell me how he was called Tonderai, twenty-eight and unemployed. They had met at her church and fallen for each other. There was nothing physical happening between them yet. She was still of that naïve age where you actually believed that it would only happen after marriage. I didn't want to tell her how hand-holding turns into kissing, that turns into something else and then bam you're fucking. That relationships sour over time is a lesson that comes with age, so who was I to burst her youthful bubble?

"Memory also has a man you know."

"No ways! How come I'm always the last to know?"

"That's because you're always so full of yourself Vimbai, trying to be a *prima donna* and all that. No one tells you stuff."

"I am not a *prima donna*." I was shocked to think the others thought that of me.

"Never mind. Anyway Memory's seeing this guy from Waterfalls but he's married."

"How can she do that?"

"She doesn't care. She says that she can share him with the wife."

I'd heard of desperate women who would take whatever they got even if it was someone else's husband, but I never thought Memory would be one of them. I was about to say this when I recalled my own past. Those in glass houses shouldn't throw stones.

Charlie Boy had a wife, so it was just me and Agnes, the singletons left. That was some company to be in. Here I was turning twenty-six and with a child. I shuddered at the thought of my birthday, which was in October, just a few months away. My prospects seemed bleak all of a sudden.

***

The next Sunday I invited Dumi to my church and he agreed to come with me. It was a Pentecostal church which hired the Cine cinema in the city centre on Sunday mornings. The service ran from ten till four. Dumi, who was raised Catholic, said he did not have the stamina to endure a long service, but it was all right because we were knocking off at one o'clock. Mrs Khumalo had tried to extend Sunday hours for her clients but had given up because everyone went to church in the morning.

The band was doing a sound check when we went in. The piercing noise of mic feedback was irritating. We sat together on the middle row in the left aisle. Seats were hard to find but at least we were early. Chiwoniso joined other children in a different part of the building where they held Sunday school.

"Why don't you guys just build a church? This is just wacky, to hold a service in a cinema where they will be showing porn soon after you're gone." Dumi spoke a little too loudly because a few heads turned round to look at him.

"They don't show porn here. Anyway we don't have the funds yet to build a church."

"But let me guess, your pastor drives a Benz and wears flashy Italian suits."

"Shhh." I had to shut him up, half regretting I had brought him in.

The fact that a building built for worldly entertainment had been converted, if only for a while, to the glorification of the Lord's name was something wonderful to me.

"I'm only joking," said Dumi, as if sensing my annoyance. He had a sensitive side to him. A part of me still fought against liking him. I felt I had to maintain an appropriate distance between us.

The music began with the soft strumming of an electric guitar followed by the drums building up slowly. A woman with the mic began to sing, 'I met the Lord by the river'. As if one entity, everyone began to sing along, we all knew the lyrics to the song. The whole place became animated with hands waving in the air, holding Bibles aloft. Dumi nodded his head and clapped his hands to the beat. There was a confident aura about him, the type that someone who knows he can fit into any circle has. I had brought people to my church before and they had been tense, but not Dumi. He was a self-assured young man.

They played three more songs before the pastor came in and stood before the microphone. Pastor Roger Mvumba had built this congregation from the ground up himself. He had been raised in a family that held traditional African beliefs. One day, when he was sixteen, he was sleeping when a voice woke him up and told him to find God. He went back to sleep and the next night the same thing happened. On the third night he heard the voice. Full of fear he asked it, "Where can I find God?" The voice told him to go to the Methodist Church, which ran a local mission. There he learnt the Bible and was baptised. Twenty years later he was living in the city, working as a messenger for the city council when he heard the voice again. This time it told him that the world was ending soon and that he should form a pure church called Forward in Faith Ministries, as all the other churches were corrupt and strayed from the truth. "How can I when I have a family to feed and I am not used to speaking in front of men?" he asked the voice. It answered, "The Lord will provide." He quit his job and went about preaching on the street. Everyone thought he had gone mad. His family was thrown onto the streets because they could no longer pay rent. For years they had to live off the generosity of relatives. Gradually people joined the church and accepted his divine ministry. The church now looked after him, giving him a home to live in and food to eat. He never forgot the hard times and always encouraged us to give tithes so that the church could feed the poor.

"I greet you in the name of Christ. Hallelujah." He bellowed from the pulpit.

"Amen!!!" The congregation replied.

"Brothers and sisters in Christ. Today I want to talk to you about morality. As a messenger of God, I cannot keep quiet. It is my duty to speak the truth. Some of you may not like it, but these are not my words, they are the words of God. The end of the world is nigh, 'The cowardly, the unbelieving, the vile, the murderers, the sexually immoral, those who practise magic arts, the idolaters and liars. They will be consigned to the fiery lake of burning sulphur. This is the second death.' Revelations 21 verse 8. The Lord will come like a thief in the night so be prepared!

"Brothers and sisters, don't you see the signs in front of your eyes? Look at Zimbabwe. Ask why the Lord is punishing us like this. It's because the whole earth has become like Babylon or Sodom and Gomorrah. There are no more moral values in people's hearts. Just coming to this church this morning, I saw many young women wearing mini-skirts. Why do they do this? They do not know it, but it is because they are sent by the devil to entice men and to lead their hearts astray. They are harlots like Jezebel and if you cannot resist, then it is better for you to pluck your eyes out so you may not see. People are having sex outside of marriage and this angers the Lord. There are people raping children and they will feel the wrath of the Lord on judgement day. Timothy 3:1-9 teaches that 'Men will be lovers of themselves in the last days.' You must be on the lookout for homosexuals and sexual deviants. Perverts shall burn. How can a man and another man sleep together? God made Adam and Eve not Adam and Steve. Can a woman and a woman make a baby?

"Be careful of those who would lead you astray from the narrow straight path which leads to the house of your father…"

It was a powerful sermon filled with the power of the Holy Spirit. I could feel his words coursing through us all and touching our very souls. When he finished we began to sing, praise and worship. People went down to have the Pastor lay his hands on them and pray for repentance. I would have wanted to stay on for much longer but Dumi nudged me.

"We have to go, otherwise we'll be late for work."

"There's still a whole hour. Work is only fifteen minutes away."

"Come on, let's get out of here. I don't want to risk it."

We gathered our bags and left. Maidei would take Chiwoniso back home. The stiff manner in which Dumi walked suggested something was not quite right. It would be a long time before I learnt why, the hard way.

Sixteen

Dumi was not himself. He seemed distracted, as if there was something on his mind. Radio music played on but Dumi didn't snap his fingers to its rhythm as he normally did. There was a mechanical efficiency to the way he did his clients' hair.

"What's the matter?" Yolanda eventually asked him.

"Nothing at all," he replied with a plastic smile.

The salon was too busy for us to push the matter. Even Charlie Boy had three men sitting on a bench waiting their turn as he gave a school-boy a funky haircut that was sure to get him turned away from school. Only Charlie Boy, whistling out of tune, was oblivious to Dumi's mood. I tried to catch my tenant's eye but he avoided me. Was there something I had done wrong?

***

At home I drank tea whilst Dumi sat on the floor with Chiwoniso helping her with her homework. It gave me a break since Maidei was illiterate. Chiwoniso was fidgeting, she would much rather have been watching TV. Dumi was patient and brought her back; where I would have shouted, he only had to speak and she obeyed. Seeing him with her, I thought he'd make a great teacher.

"Uncle Dumi, can I go to bed now?"

"Not until you finish your reading. There are only two pages left."

There was a gentle authority in his tone.

"But I'm sleepy."

He got her to finish and even made her read an extra page. Then he signed the brown card that told the teacher how far she'd reached with her book. At the kind of school I'd been to, we hardly had any homework and when we did, half the time the teachers didn't check it. Admiral Tait Primary was a school that people from my home neighborhood could only dream of. The teachers knew what they were doing and the library had the right books for my daughter to read. It was expensive though, and I dreaded what would happen when she finally reached high school. If I didn't get my life sorted soon, she'd be forced into a former group B school in the high-density areas: a sure-fire way to flunk and get pregnant before she was nineteen. There were nights when I couldn't sleep worrying that my baby would not have the sort of future she deserved.

After I'd put Chiwoniso to bed I returned to the living room. The TV was showing a local drama. Dumi was on his favorite sofa, his eyes glued to the screen, but I could tell he was not watching it. I sat closer to him and decided to engage him.

"I know something's wrong. You haven't been yourself all day."

"We should subscribe to DSTV, the ZBC stuff is crap." He tried to deflect me.

"Is it something I've done?"

"I mean this drama is twenty years old and they will keep repeating it."

"Dumisani, I'm trying to help."

"I don't need any help!" he shouted and got up, going to his bedroom and banging the door behind him.

The sound of chirping crickets was the neighbourhood lullaby. Exactly why they had to rub their hind legs together just below my window, was something I didn't try to understand. The noise seemed only marginally preferable to a whining mosquito waiting to bite you. I tossed and turned. The room was very hot but I didn't dare open the window in case I let mosquitoes in.

I figured out that I couldn't get to sleep unless I understood the source of Dumi's bad mood so I got up and knocked on his door.

"Come in."

"Hey, are you still awake?"

"No, you've just woken me," he said, but his voice was not in the least drowsy. He was lying on the bed scribbling in a small black book.

"Sorry." I was trying not to be distracted by the sight of his naked chiselled torso. The boy had a six-pack!

"It's all right, I wasn't really asleep anyway. I've just been listening to the crickets, it was driving me insane."

"Me too," I laughed. "Don't think I'm trying to pressure you but seeing that we're living under the same roof makes us virtually family, and I'm just concerned about whatever's on your mind. You should know that you can talk to me about anything."

He sighed. His room was even tidier than my own. Everything was very well ordered, even though the number of his possessions should have resulted in clutter. I stood by the door until he gestured for me to come in and sit on a stool by the dressing table. I was mindful enough to keep the door wide open. There was a distant look in his eyes as if he was thinking of something profound. It was best to wait until he was ready to speak. My limited experience with men had taught me that much.

"This is going to seem very silly to you."

"It's not silly if it's bothering you this much."

He took a deep breath, and looked like a fish gasping for breath in the open air. "My elder brother, Patrick, is getting married next week Saturday."

"That's great news." I was a sucker for weddings and figured he might be a bit grumpy because he was struggling with getting a present or something like that.

"The thing is, I fell out with my family twelve months ago and we haven't spoken since."

I know all about falling out with family so I said, "I take it you're wondering whether or not you should go to the wedding."

"How did you know?"

"It's obvious. I would be asking myself the same thing if I were in your position."

"I don't know what to do."

"If you want my opinion, I think you should go." I felt a bit like an agony aunt. "It's your brother, we only live once and you'll regret not having been there on his wedding day for the rest of your life if you choose to stay away."

He snuggled his head into the pillow and looked at the ceiling while I stifled a yawn.

"That's just the thing, that's what I want, but to do it is hard."

"A wise man once told me to swallow my pride," I said, thinking of Fungai.

"It's not a matter of pride…"

"You should go."

"I will go," he said suddenly, with a half smile. "Thanks, Vimbai. I guess I just needed someone to tell me that."

I got up happy that I had done what I could to help him. The parallel with my own family problems was disturbing and I just prayed that things would work out better for him. Before I left I turned round and asked, "What was the problem between you and the family?"

"It was just something stupid… Please switch off the light on your way out."

Seventeen

There are people that can get anything they want through the strength of their personality. It's a combination of having the right type of education and an upbringing that taught you how to navigate society's mores. It was on Monday morning that Mrs Khumalo gathered us together for a special announcement. She was smiling at us, something we were unused to. This sort of meeting was not something we had ever had before so we sat down and waited in nervous anticipation.

"There are going to be some new developments," she said. "Next month we're going to shut down the salon for a time (*I had a sinking feeling in my stomach at the thought of going without pay*). You will be paid your full salaries, of course, (*I felt better straight away*) because it's a result of all your hard work that this salon is now doing so well. There should be no doubt in anyone's mind that we are the best in the city. So, we have decided to do some extensive renovations and expand the building. If we are Number One then we have to look the part."

We clapped our hands enthusiastically and congratulated each other. Mrs Khumalo reached from behind the cash desk and brought out a bottle of champagne, which she poured into seven plastic tumblers.

"I also have one more very important notification." (*Mrs Khumalo loved big words*). "I've been running this place with your help, but I have many other responsibilities. This place needs a manager. It needs someone who is responsible and has experience in the industry. Agnes is my daughter but that is not a qualification in itself. There are two people I have had to choose between. Vimbai has many years of experience and is very good with our clients. They all know her and respect her, and for many years she has shouldered the responsibility of making sure the standard of our work is world class. I also know she is hardworking and loyal. The other person is Dumisani. He has less experience but he's innovative and creative. It was a tough choice for me, and I couldn't sleep, but my decision is … Dumisani, because he has dynamism and an X-factor that I can't quite articulate. Raise your glasses."

My mind went blank. My hand limply raised the cup as if by some supernatural force. All my years of loyal service down the drain. Agnes gave me a satanic smile. Yolanda and Memory looked sympathetic as if they were torn in two. Charlie Boy smiled enthusiastically.

"I would like to declare a toast to the salon and to our manager Dumisani."

I tipped the drink down my throat. This was the first time I'd drunk champagne. Its bubbles tingled my tongue but I downed it with a gulp, and found it unpalatable. I squeezed the cup so hard it broke with the characteristic plastic snap. The others were clapping but my hands only moved when Yolanda elbowed me. Dumisani got up and gestured for us to be still. I figured he wanted to test his new powers.

"Well," he said, "I wasn't expecting this when I came in to work this morning. Thank you, Mrs Khumalo, I am well and truly humbled. I just want to say to the rest of the team (*team – what was this? did he think we were some sort of rugby squad?*) that we must work well together. I can't do this alone; I'm going to need your help to make sure that this business continues to be a success. If there are any problems or issues, please do not hesitate to see me, my door is always open (*you don't even have a bloody office*). That's all I have to say, now let's get to work, people."

The two of them left the room grinning at each other like two civet cats. No doubt they were going out to discuss his pay increase. Less than six months after he had started, he was manager. I felt like resigning on the spot. I even took a half-hearted step forward and then sank back in my chair.

"Tough luck, *shamwari*," Agnes said with a contemptuous laugh.

"*Nxii*, I didn't want the job anyway," I replied.

"Then why are your eyes so red? I think someone is jealous."

"Come on, that's not nice. Leave her alone." Yolanda stood up for me, something I will be grateful for for the rest of my life, because if she hadn't, Lord only knows what I would have done.

Dazed for the rest of the day, I worked like an automaton, without an ounce of life left in me.

"Are you going to wait for me while I do the cash and lock up? It will only take two minutes," Dumi said when, at last, the day ended.

"There's something important I need to do at home." I grabbed my bag and dragged my feet, which felt as if they had lead weights attached to them.

Car brakes screeched as a car came to a sudden halt in front of me.

"You stupid idiot, how can you step into the middle of the road! Are you mad or something?" The driver waved his fist, his face contorted. People were staring at me as I hurried off. The driver shouted some obscenities and drove away. I walked into Harare Gardens, the once lovely botanical masterpiece that now looked exactly how I felt. The rows of once neat flowers were wilted and the lawn was a brown desert. On the benches lay the homeless soaking up the sun. Amidst this squalor was a blue uniformed ice-cream man ringing his bell, trying to entice people to buy a cone. A pot-bellied man who looked as if he needed a shave was going in the opposite direction when he turned around suddenly saying, "God must be missing an angel, because girl when I saw you, I knew you must be one of his angels."

I ignored him.

"You must be a hell of a thief because you stole my heart just by the way you walk." He was trotting, trying to catch up with me. "Girl, talk to me, just for a minute and I will be happy for the rest of my life… hell baby you are hard to get but let me be your Romeo and I'll treat you like the princess you are."

"Go away," I said increasing my pace.

"Baby, just give me a chance, I'm a great guy, I have a good job, my own house and a nice car. It's just at the garage today that's why I'm walking.

"I'm not interested."

"I know you're not but I am. Tell you what, give me your phone number and I'll call you. We can get to know each other. How about it?"

"Leave me alone you pervert!" I shouted so loudly that all the people around us could hear. He got the message and stopped. Then the barrage I was waiting for came: "You slut, I was just trying to give you a chance, do you really think anyone in their right mind would want to go out with something as ugly as you…"

I kept walking and didn't look back. Tears ran down my cheeks streaking my make-up. I was crying in public and I didn't care. All I needed was to get home to be with my daughter. I passed by the Reserve Bank and stopped to look at my face in the windows. Seeing my face, I felt ugly. I was a puny ugly insect standing at the base of one of the tallest buildings in the city, which the likes of me could never hope to ascend.

The city went on with its business as usual oblivious to my pain. This is what it was to be a single mother, ugly and without prospects. I made my way to the bus stop, brushing past bodies, praying that somehow the earth would swallow me up.

Eighteen

It was only when I had Chiwoniso in my arms that I felt life was worth living again. Her tiny head on my bosom filled me with a strength that was like a good drug coursing through my veins. There is no way she could understand why I was holding her so close, but I was slipping and she was the only thing stopping me from going over the edge. I let her go and she went off to her bedroom to play with her toys. Smoke was coming into the house so I told Maidei to shut the kitchen door.

It would have been nice to soak myself in the bath but the geyser was switched off and it would take time for the water to warm up. I walked to the radio and looked at the pile of CDs. I put on Joe Thomas's 'All That I Am', and remembered when he'd come to Zimbabwe for a tour. I removed it when he started to go on about love. I needed something to chill me out, not some romantic crap.

There was the sound of keys in the door and then Dumi came in. He threw himself on the sofa and said, "What a day, hey?"

"Um hum." I couldn't be asked to waste my breath.

"We need to talk."

"About what?" Why wouldn't he just go away?

"I just think we should talk about what happened at work today." He seemed a little timorous.

"You may be the manager but that doesn't mean we should bring work home. This is my house and don't you forget it."

"That's not what I was on about. I just need to know there are no hard feelings that's all."

"Why should there be?" I swatted a mosquito that settled on the wall next to me. It burst leaving a bloody smudge.

"I just think that you've worked at the salon for much longer than any of us and if I were you I would feel some sort of entitlement when this post came up."

"Maybe you should tell that to the boss."

"I'll resign tomorrow then," he said getting up, "Our friendship means more to me than some stupid job."

"Don't be silly." I was stunned he considered me a friend and was willing to make this sacrifice for my happiness. "I think you'll be a great manager."

"That means a lot to me. Look what I've got." He fished out two bottles of Green Valley wine.

Forward in Faith Ministries forbade the drinking of alcohol but I thought to hell with it and drank anyway. I needed something to drown my sorrows. The sweet wine went quickly to my head. I hadn't eaten, so I was drinking on an empty stomach.

"There was something else I wanted to talk to you about," said Dumi.

"Here we go again."

"It's about the wedding."

"Don't tell me you've changed your mind again."

"I wouldn't do such a thing, but I have a problem. I had a date for Saturday but it turns out she has other plans, so I was wondering if you could come with me."

"What will your girlfriend think?"

"She's a girl and a friend but not my girlfriend."

"Why don't you go with your girlfriend whoever she is then?"

He shrugged and said, "That would be very difficult given the fact that I don't have a girlfriend."

A guy like him being single was next to impossible. He should have had a girlfriend. In fact, now I thought about it, I'd never seen him make a pass at any of the girls at work or anywhere else at that. Flirting with the clients seemed like second nature to him but he always held back and kept things professional. I'd just assumed he had a girlfriend or girlfriends...

"You should go with Yolanda. I think she likes you."

"There's no way I'm taking her. Her boyfriend is massive. I'm too young to die."

"What about Memory?"

"She's a great girl but I need someone who knows how to carry themselves amongst people they don't know."

"And you think I know how to carry myself?" I was intrigued and flattered at the same time.

"You're classy and good looking. I need a piece of eye candy dangling off the side of my arm." He laughed and threw his hands wide open. "How about it?"

"I'll have to think about it."

"Oh come now, the wedding is Saturday and I'm not taking no for an answer." That settled the matter. I might have been bitter but I've always loved weddings and it would be the first one this year. I wasn't going to resist any further.

***

On Friday we got off early. Dumi arranged the books so we had few clients in the shop and left Agnes in charge. The two of us made our way to Parirenyatwa hospital where we caught a kombi. It was early in the afternoon, so we actually had a whole seat to ourselves. The vehicle wove slowly along avoiding the potholes. It was a rickety old thing and Dumi said if it hit one more pothole the suspension would give. We went past Avondale, with its antiquated charms. There was life all around us, people walking the streets as if they had jobs.

The kombi stopped and picked up two girls wearing extra-large sunglasses who spoke in English with a nasal accent. Back in the day they would have been called *manose* brigade; anything that stripped you of your Africanness – whether it was the sound of your voice or the nature of your hair – was something to be admired. One day perhaps Chiwoniso would speak like these girls. Maybe it was progress, but it didn't feel right.

"Shit, when did they set that up!" The driver slammed on his brakes for a roadblock.

Three policemen lazily waved the cars in front of us through but stopped our kombi and told the driver to park near the pavement, where another policeman sat in the shade, a rifle placed across his lap.

"Is this car registered?" the officer asked once he had greeted the driver.

"Hongu ishe." The driver nodded his head vigorously.

The policeman went round the car kicking each tyre as he went. He gave me a perverted look but went past without molesting us. When he was back at the driver's door, he whistled and shook his head. "This commuter omnibus is unroadworthy. The tyres have no treads, in fact they're bald; there are no reflectors on your mudguard, and your wipers have no blades on them. This car is a death trap. I am sure if we take it down to the VID, they will find more problems. I have no choice but to impound it."

"This car is my livelihood. If you take it away my family will starve." The driver was clapping his hands and pleading with the policeman.

"I feel sorry for you, but I just have no choice. Public safety is not something we can toy around with. Just last week a kombi over-turned on the Harare-Masvingo road because the brake pads were worn out and the driver could not stop in time. Ask your passengers to step out of the vehicle."

"Please, I'm begging you, don't take my car away."

"I'm just following the law," the officer said, folding his hands.

"Please, there must be something you can do." The driver's voice was cracking.

"Help me to help you," the officer said in the quietest of voices.

That was all the prompting the driver needed. He knew what to do. He took a large wad of banknotes and handed it to the policeman who pocketed it in a slow casual movement.

"I'm only doing this as an act of kindness; you have to get the problems on your car fixed. Next time, be quick to produce the right paperwork." The policeman waved us through and we left, the kombi churning out copious amounts of smoke as it took off.

***

This was my first time at the Westgate Shopping Centre since it opened in the late nineties. Its immaculate pinkish walls and the litter-free pavements made it feel like something from a first-world Mediterranean country. The people who shopped here also had a sophistication about them. They wore beautiful clothes and ate ice-cream. There were so many shops, all fully stocked. It was a woman's paradise. The only thing that put me off were the prices. I couldn't believe that people paid them, but there were plenty of customers with heaving shopping bags making their way to their flashy cars.

"Over here." Dumi led me into a tiny boutique full of fashionable clothes that were clearly imported. Seeing us enter, the shopkeeper leapt up. "Hey, Dumisani. Long time, man. I thought you didn't want to come here any more."

"How could I not? This is the best shop in the country."

"Business is slow, man."

"That's because people don't know quality. My brother Patrick is getting married tomorrow and the two of us need clothes."

"You've come to the right place. I'll show the lady around. You know your way around the shop – just grab whatever you like."

The storekeeper showed me several dresses that were all my size, each lovelier than the last. I settled on a strapless red dress with a corsage that was labelled 'red organza rose corsage prom dress'.

"You've made a fine choice. It came in just last week from Paris," the salesman told me.

Dumi showed him the tuxedo he'd chosen and the attendant responded in a weird voice, "Oh suit yourself, sir," then packed up laughing at the joke which I didn't get. The dress was put in a box and the suit packed.

"I heard about Colin's departure. I'm so sorry. They're clamping down on us. We have to be extra careful, bro," the salesman said quietly as he wrapped the packages.

"Everything happens for a reason," Dumi replied, looking at me.

"I know, but it must be difficult for you. The two of you were close like this." He crossed two fingers on his right hand.

"Just tell me the price." I thought I saw a brief flash of what may have been unease on Dumi's face, but when I looked again, there was nothing to indicate that anything was wrong.

I could have choked when the attendant gave us the bill. The suit and the dress cost thirty-nine times more than what each of us earned in a month. Dumi didn't seem phased.

"That's not too bad."

"Are you going to put it on the account?" the young man asked with an edgy smile.

"Of course." Dumi signed a ledger that was suddenly there in front of him. We took the clothes and headed out. I couldn't help turning back, worried that I had been drawn into some sort of con, but Dumi was his usual breezy confident self.

When I asked how he could afford to buy us all this gear, he refused to answer, mumbling something vague about how he had an account. We bought ice-cream and sat in the shade of a palm tree by the cinema court fountain. Four bronze elephants shot jets of water through their trunks into the blue pool. People walked by with their expensive shopping. I dreamt of myself in the red dress. In a few weeks I would come to understand where Dumi got the money from.

Nineteen

The Ncubes had four children, three boys and a girl, the youngest. Dumisani was the third child; Patrick was the first-born. The weather was clear with wispy cirrus clouds floating in the sky. The wedding was taking place at the Catholic cathedral and I was worried that my dress would be crumpled on the commute. Despite Dumi's desperate pleas, we let three kombis go by until we caught one that was sufficiently empty.

Twice I had to stop him from chewing his fingernails. His eyes had a vacant stare as if he was fearful of something. I'd never seen him this agitated.

"It's going to be just fine. They'll be happy to see you."

"I hope so. I reckon I'll melt like a vampire when we get inside the church." Dumi stared through the window at the buildings as we went past. The tuxedo he'd chosen was a three-piece black single-breasted Worcester that looked like something one only saw on television. It had a platinum coloured waistcoat and a matching tie with elegant designs. It even had a matching handkerchief in the breast pocket. While I fretted with my dress, he looked comfortable and at ease. I fancied other girls seeing me arrive with him would be envious, and that made me nervous. What if he walked away from me during the wedding; what would I do?

"Promise you'll stay beside me all day."

"You'll be fine." He looked into my eyes when he said that and it made me feel better.

When we got to the church on Fourth Street, the service had already begun. A spotty teenager with a badge labelled 'usher' led us to a seat in the pews. This was my first time in the Cathedral, though I had passed by it often. The stone masonry with its twin bell towers was an obvious European imitation, another heritage of our colonial past. The interior was cool and a gentle breeze blew through the open windows.

The priest was dressed in elaborate robes and he droned on in a pleasing voice as if this was something he'd done a thousand times before.

"That's the archbishop," Dumi whispered in my ear. I'd never seen an archbishop before and I expected him to be white, but he was even darker than me.

I'd been told that Catholic masses were stale and cold with dull organ music so I was surprised when the choir broke into song. They sang in Shona, with African drums and rattles, *ngoma ne hosho*. The women's voices merged with the men's bass producing an effect that was confusing but beautiful. At Forward in Faith Ministries we only used guitars, western drums and a keyboard, because Pastor Mavumba preached against using traditional African instruments. He said that before the missionaries came, our people engaged in devil worship, so the instruments they used were the devil's instruments. We sang in English and he preached in English too, when he was not speaking in tongues. I was a bit confused; maybe the Catholic Church was the devil's church after all, but I couldn't stop my foot tapping along to the music.

The Archbishop moved on to the vows. I could not see the couple properly because there were so many heads in front of us and they stood a step below the Archbishop. From the front row I could hear a woman weeping. I didn't know if she was the bride's mother or the groom's. Tears glistened in Dumi's eyes as he heard his brother make his vows. Later I was to learn that with divorce not tolerated by the

Catholics, it gave the ceremony a more solemn air than anything I'd seen before.

The whole congregation erupted in applause and ululation once the vows had been made. Dumi took my hand in his and squeezed it and I saw tears of joy in his eyes.

"That's my brother." He pointed unneccessarily to the groom and his bride walking slowly down the aisle of the church. Patrick looked just like Dumi except rather more mature. The bride was stunning and her wedding dress had such a long train that it took six flower-girls to carry it, which they did with great reverence. They were followed by the best man, maid of honour, and a dozen bridesmaids and groomsmen. The bridesmaids all wore pink strapless dresses of such filigreed material, they could have been wedding dresses without trains. They carried hand-tied bouquets interlaced with Swarovski crystals and ribbons the colour of candy floss. The groomsmen wore tail tuxedos complete with top hats and tiny canes with brass knobs, which they carried with self-conscious airs. My mind was trying to work out how much the clothes alone cost, billions, trillions, when Dumi pointed, "There are my parents," but amidst all the people in the wedding party, I could not quite make out which couple he was referring to.

It took a while for us to leave the church because the ushers conducted the guests from the front pews first. When we finally made it, the wedding party had left. They were being whisked off to Lake Chivero for their wedding photos. Shouldn't Dumisani have been with them?

"You're going to love the reception. That's the best bit of the wedding," Dumisani said cheerfully.

A man shouted out to him, "Cousin Dumi, what the hell are you doing here. You missed the cars going to the photo shoot." They shook hands.

We were surrounded by people greeting him and congratulating him on his brother's wedding. Most of them were relatives and friends. He spoke with everyone in a familiar manner, like someone used to being the centre of attention. I stood behind him like a stooge not knowing what to do with myself. Some of the guests came to have their picture taken with him.

I tugged his sleeve and he turned back.

"Remember me?"

"Don't be silly, Vimbai. I just want every one to wonder who the stunner is that I've brought with me." He took my hand. "We need transport to the reception."

"Where's it going to be?" I asked.

"My parents' house. Stay here for a minute, I have to find us a lift."

He vanished and I was left on my own watching the guests milling about. My mouth was dry, a sure sign that I was nervous. I wasn't used to hanging around with people that I didn't know. I scanned the crowd trying to pick out a familiar face, but I couldn't find one. Everyone was new to me and everyone was well dressed. The air was filled with perfumes that I'd never smelt before and I felt like going to each of the finely dressed ladies to ask them what brand they wore. Pointless. I could never afford them anyway.

A minute later Dumisani returned. Before he reached me another man stopped him and chatted briefly before letting him go.

"I thought you said you wouldn't leave me alone." I was fighting to control my temper.

"Sorry, I just had to try to get us a ride. All the cars are full just now but my cousin Mike will be back for us in thirty, maybe forty-five minutes." He looked into my eyes making me feel like I was the only person that mattered.

Slowly everyone melted away until we were among just a few people left waiting for our lift. My feet hurt in my high heels. I could not afford to soil my dress by sitting on a dirty bench so I just endured the pain of my pinched toes. It seemed chivalrous that Dumisani stood with me, impatiently shifting his weight from one foot to the other. There was nothing for us to do but watch the slow-moving traffic. A vendor trying his luck came up to try to sell freezits and maputi, but no one was buying.

"Can I ask you something?" I said to Dumi.

"Sure thing."

"I don't want you to take this the wrong way."

"It's a bit difficult to take something the wrong way if you haven't heard it."

"I just need to know why you lied to me that your parents were so poor you had to get a scholarship to get through high school." I was hoping he wouldn't be offended, so I was relieved when he laughed.

"Dear me, I never said my parents were poor. I only said that I went through school on a rugby scholarship."

I felt a bit of an idiot, but luckily cousin Mike's Lexus pulled up. I was about to learn just how affluent Dumi's parents really were.

Twenty

The electric gates swung open slowly and we drove up a long winding driveway until we reached the house atop a little hill. Cousin Mike struggled to find parking in the carport because there was an assortment of smart cars tightly packed together: Mercedes, BMWs, Escalades, Audis, all manner of 4x4's and even a solitary Hummer. Cousin Mike found a parking spot in the bushes as if embarrassed by his car.

Dumi got out and opened the door for me. I hesitated but he reached out his hand and I stepped out feeling like Cinderella wondering just how much time I had before I turned into a pumpkin. Dumi could tell I was nervous.

"Relax, they don't bite."

"Can we wait for two minutes."

"Go on ahead. We'll be with you in two minutes," Dumi said to cousin Mike.

"Just give me a shout if you need anything."

When Mike had left I nervously rearranged my dress.

"You look lovely."

"I've never been so nervous in my whole life." I flashed an edgy smile. "Maybe you should've brought someone else with you."

"There's no one I'd rather be with today. Remember that you and

I are millionaires. Come now, let's go inside."

The house was a mansion with a thatched roof, oiled beams, and built of granite and glass. The floors were tiled in marble and there was a fishpond with goldfish in the entrance hall where people were standing around sipping champagne.

"Dumisani my son! Come here!" shouted a man who was already inebriated.

"Uncle Thomas, it's been such a long time." The two embraced enthusiastically.

"And who is this fine young creature you have brought with you?"

"This is Vimbai, we work together.'

"If only I were forty years younger... Don't tell your aunt I said that." He kissed both my cheeks and I could smell the whisky on his breath.

We were grabbed by a host of people who wanted to greet us. There were cousins, friends, business associates, church members and all manner of others mingling and celebrating. I shook a hundred hands and kissed twice that number of lips which was not the traditional way. All this time Dumi kept me firmly at his side and I felt secure. A maid in a black and white dress with a ridiculous little hat came and asked if I wanted a drink. I requested a glass of water for myself and some orange juice for Dumi.

"Let's go outside for a bit of fresh air," Dumi said after a while. Perhaps he was as tired as I was of listening to the lame jokes.

We stepped out through massive French doors. The swimming pool had been hewn into the bedrock, which served as the foundation to the house. The solar powered pool engine hummed in the background.

"Look how the water seems to disappear over the edge as if it were extending into the horizon It's called an infinity pool. Dad had engineers, architects and all sorts of people come over just to make sure it was done right. Of course it's heated at night but no one ever seems to use it. Such a waste."

"It's beautiful."

We walked down towards the edge of the pool from where there was a breathtaking view of the valley below. "That house over there belongs to Strive Masiyiwa, the guy who owns Econet. Maybe you should ask him for unlimited airtime when he stops by later." We were surrounded by trees and I could hear birds singing. I felt I was in the countryside. There was a clay tennis court just below us and I was enjoying the view when I saw two soldiers in camouflage squatting in the bushes.

"What are those soldiers doing?" My heart pumped, remembering how people had been beaten in the streets by soldiers during the last election.

"You mean those guys, or maybe those ones, or those guys over there?" The place was packed with them. "I don't know, there must be someone important coming. Don't worry, they're harmless."

There had been soldiers in the streets and some manning the gate when we came in but I hadn't given it any thought before now.

The wedding party came in just after three o'clock. I could see Dumisani tense up as if the prospect of meeting his family was unbearable. We walked towards them but had to wait as they were having photos taken in the garden.

"The prodigal son returns," said Patrick with a huge smile. "You've no idea what it means to us to see you here, bro. I didn't think you'd come but Tsungi said you would make it and you did." The bride, Tsungi, gave Dumi a kiss and the three of them embraced.

"I wouldn't have missed this for the world."

The whole family embraced in one large group hug around Dumisani. It was as if by clinging to him they were trying to exorcise a demon that had plagued the family. The tenderness there almost moved me to tears.

"What have we here?" said a short man with a moustache and a shiny bald head.

"Dad, I want you to meet my girlfriend, Vimbai," said Dumi. I was taken aback. He had called me his girlfriend. How was I to respond?

"Your girlfriend?" repeated his mother, a tall woman who must have been a beauty in her prime. Then she burst into tears. I thought I had done something wrong, but how could I, just by standing there? Maybe I wasn't good enough for her son? Why should that even matter? I was not really his girlfriend. Should I correct the mistake? "Come here, my child," she said, and embraced me.

The whole family gathered around me like I was some sort of zoological curiosity. They prodded and felt me, as if to check if I really was really flesh and blood. I said, "*Makadini henyu,*" clapped my hands and curtsied in the traditional manner.

"See that! She is well-mannered, not like these modern girls walking the streets of Harare," his father cried triumphantly. The bride cast me a jealous glare as if I was stealing her show. A short skinny bridesmaid wearing spectacles pushed her way to the front. She introduced herself as Michelle, Dumisani's younger sister.

"Get off her, people, you're suffocating her. God, she must think we're a family of weirdos." She grabbed my wrist. "Let's get out of here."

"Wait please. Let's get a photo taken with her," Dumi's father said.

If my day had ended then, with me on cloud nine, it would have been a success and I would have been saved from the embarrassment of what happened later that evening.

***

Michelle and I hit it off at once. She was nineteen and had very white teeth, which dazzled you when she smiled. For a skinny girl she had bumps in all the right places. She whisked me off to her bedroom, which was twice as large as my living room. Whilst there she interrogated me about how I'd met her brother, how we got on and the like. I answered the questions truthfully, we had met at the hair salon where we both worked, we got on well, etc. She didn't delve any deeper into the relationship and so I was grateful that I didn't have to answer any more personal questions until I had figured out just where Dumi and I were going with this

"Let's go down. We have to meet and greet otherwise people will say we're arrogant twats." Michelle had a southern twang that was the result of having done her schooling in the USA.

There were even more people down at the party, a mixture of blacks and whites, and I heard a number of foreign accents. I got to rub shoulders with men like Nigel Chanakira, Mutumwa Mawere,

Jonathan Moyo, Nicholas van Hoogstraten and a host of others from the business and the political world. Now I understood why the security was so tight.

"Auntie Grace!" squealed Michelle, running over to hug a familiar looking lady wearing a large veiled hat that looked like she was going to the races at Ascot. I racked my brain trying to remember just where I had met her before. "Auntie Grace, I want you to meet my *muroora* Vimbai."

The lady shook my hand and kissed my cheeks. As she did so I gave an involuntary whimper, realising I was being kissed by the president's wife.

"How do you do my child?"

I stammered, unable to speak.

"Vimbai is the best hairdresser in the country. You should let her do your hair and maybe you'll stop hiding it beneath those hats of yours," Michelle joked. I didn't know whether to laugh and only did so when the first lady laughed.

"If she is as good as you say then I would love that. Ring my office and we can arrange an appointment."

Michelle led me away without my having said a single word. 'The first lady wants me to do her hair' spun in my head. I was in seventh heaven, when a familiar face came up to me.

"Vimbai, what on earth are you doing here?" It was Phillip, as drunk as a fish, and bumping through the guests as he staggered towards us. "Hello darling."

He tried to kiss me and I moved away.

"*Wavakuvhaira manje.* It must be because you're mixing with the great and the good." He spilt beer on the floor, trying to keep his balance.

I swallowed hard and stared at the floor.

"Hey, come on baby, what's the matter?" He leaned over, unsteady on his feet, spilling beer on my brand new dress. As I tried to back away he grabbed my backside.

"Let her go, you creep," said Michelle trying to prise me loose. People were beginning to stare. Phillip shoved her hard and she went flying across the floor.

"This is my whore, you should all know it!" he shouted at the top of his voice. I started to cry. I had never been so humiliated in my life.

Dumi and his brother Luke appeared from nowhere. Dumi set me loose and punched Phillip in the face. The bully landed hard on the marble floor and spat out both front teeth. A woman screamed. The two brothers yanked their victim up and bundled him out of the room, leaving a trail of blood on the floor behind them. It seemed impossible that they had defended the honour of a girl from Budiriro, when she'd been affronted by one of the wealthiest and best-connected businessmen in the country. Guests were talking and pointing at me as if I was a circus freak.

Michelle led me out of the room and guided me back to her bedroom. She kept asking if I was all right and if I needed anything. I told her I just wanted to go home. For ten minutes she tried to convince me to stay, but I couldn't face all those people again. A chauffeur drove me home, and I felt more like Cinderella than ever.

Twenty-One

It should have rained for me on Monday, but it didn't. As if to mock me the sun shone in all its glory and there was not a single cloud in the sky. I had a sick feeling in the pit of my stomach. It was the sort of feeling you have when you've thrown up so much and there isn't anything left in your stomach but you keep retching. I saw Chiwoniso off with a kiss and went back to bed. There was a chance I would be sacked but I didn't care. I tossed and turned for a bit replaying the events at the wedding for the hundredth time. Meeting all those wonderful people and then bam, Phillip came along like a bull.

If it weren't for Chiwoniso, I would regret ever having met him, but she was undeniably the one good that had come out of it all. The man hadn't spoken to me in months and then he puts his grimy hands around me as if I'm a piece of furniture. When I closed my eyes I saw all the guests looking and pointing at me and felt even sicker.

I had sense enough at ten o'clock to pick up the phone and call Mrs Khumalo. If I was going to get sacked then at least I should get it over and done with.

"Hello," she answered on a crackly line.

"I'm not feeling well. I can't come in to work today." I wasn't lying, I felt horrible.

"You should talk to Dumi, he's your manager."

What an idea! I couldn't bear to speak with him. He hadn't come home on Sunday and I feared the worst.

"I tried to call the salon but the phone was engaged."

"It should be all right. Take all the time you need, my dear. See you at work tomorrow.' She hung up.

I closed the curtains and crawled back into bed. Maidei brought me a cup of tea, which I left on the sideboard until it grew cold. I felt worse than a drug addict coming down from a high. I shut my eyes and drifted in and out of consciousness. All I needed was someone with a gun to put me out of my misery.

***

My phone rang. It was a number I didn't know so I let it ring out. It rang again and then again. I gave up and answered it.

"Hello, is this Vimbai? It's Michelle, I'm driving up and down Clyde Road like a lunatic. I've knocked on two wrong houses already, which one is your place?"

"Number 10, that's the one with a black gate, you can't miss it."

"Thanks." She hung up.

I jumped out of bed and looked for something presentable to wear. She was tooting at the gate, so I sent Maidei to open it for her. The wardrobe was full of clean clothes but none of them seemed good enough. My hair was a mess and I could hear them coming into the house.

"*Tisvikewo,*" Michelle said, which sounded funny in her American accent.

"Just give me two minutes," I called out.

"I'm going to tell my parents that their *muroora* is so lazy she sleeps until one in the afternoon."

I pulled on a pair of blue jeans and a white shirt and tied my hair back in a ponytail. That would have to do for the time being. I rushed out and greeted her. She rose and kissed my cheeks.

"Welcome to my house Make yourself feel at home."

Maidei came out with a glass of diluting juice and I sent her back to get some Coke instead.

"This is a nice house you have here," Michelle said, looking around.

"You can't say that, you live in a palace." I was flattered.

"Really it is nice and cosy. I can see why Dumi moved in here." I remained silent. It would reflect badly on me if they thought that we were already living together as a couple, especially with the scene Phillip had caused at the party. She could tell I was uncomfortable, so she added, "When I was in Memphis I lived with an older guy for three months, but we broke up before I came back. He found it tough to be with me because I made him do all the cooking and cleaning. I told him in Africa we have maids, so I wasn't used to it. He must have got scared at the prospect of a lifetime with me and so he ran."

I laughed, relieved she was sharing her dirty little secret with me.

"What was it like in America?"

"It's all right but its nothing like home. The people there don't wash." She got up, moved over to the radio and looked at my CD collection. "This music is sooo old."

"Those are the classics," I retorted.

"Who listens to Tevin Campell or K- Ci and Jojo any more?" She put the CDs neatly back in their place.

Chiwoniso came running in and jumped on me. She was still in her uniform and her satchel dangled on her back.

"Mummy, I'm hungry."

"And who do we have here?" Michelle moved forward, offering her hand.

"This is my daughter, Chiwoniso." My heart fluttered. They would never accept me if they knew I already had a child, and, worse, one born out of wedlock. I felt my heart sink even as I looked at my precious baby.

"Oh my God she's so cute. Come here, come to Auntie Michelle." Picking her up, Michelle brought Chiwoniso over to the sofa next to me. They were smiling at each other and holding hands. "Why didn't you tell me you had a daughter? I'm feeling sooo broody now. Look at her."

This reaction took me by surprise. If I hadn't composed myself I would have gasped. The inevitable question followed.

"Who's the father?"

I buried my head in my hands. "You don't want to know."

"Of course I do, and if he's single I'm getting myself a sperm donation." She laughed as if this was the most natural thing to say in the world.

"Phillip Mabayo."

"That jackass! Hell no, I aint going there." We both laughed. "So that explains why he was being such a prick at the wedding."

I told her how I hadn't seen Phillip in ages and that there'd been nothing between us for years. Michelle was a good listener and very sympathetic when she learnt that he had reneged on his responsibilities as a father. We laughed at the thought of Phillip losing his two front teeth.

"Every time he speaks it will sound like th, th, th." Michelle said. Even at nineteen she was of the same opinion as I was that all men were pigs. She could not take her eyes off Chiwoniso and in my relief, I felt happy, but Michelle was just one person. What of the whole family? I wondered if they would all be so open-minded.

"Dumi never came back home on Saturday." I was anxious to find out the extent of the damage Phillip had inflicted.

"It's not because of Phillip." That reassured me. "Patrick and Tsungai were leaving for their honeymoon in Jamaica on Sunday, so we all had to be there to see them off at the airport. He might stay over for a few more days just for us to catch up on things."

"Why did he fall out with the rest of the family? He's such a nice guy that I find it hard to believe he would ever fall out with anyone. At least not intentionally."

"All families squabble. I was in America when it happened. It was probably nothing, but Dumi is a sensitive guy. The important thing is that we are together now as a family... plus you of course. You're going to be my best friend in the whole wide world."

Charm must have been a genetic trait in the Ncube family. Michelle had made me feel better from the moment I'd met her.

We talked about a lot of things. I found myself wondering if this was real or a façade. Dumi had said I was his girlfriend but we'd never spoken about having a relationship. If it was a game how far should I play along with it? Why were we playing it in the first place? I needed answers.

Twenty-two

Tuesday was the first day of September and I went to work with my spirits high. The cramped commuter and the abusive conductor did nothing to dampen my spirits. There was a light drizzle as if the rain was teasing the earth. I passed several banks with long winding queues, feeling lucky that I was paid in cash, and so never had to endure the soul-destroying hours waiting in line for your own money.

I looked forward to seeing Dumi, though I was a little apprehensive. The way in which Michelle had spoken to me did a lot to reassure me that everything would be all right. When I arrived Dumi was opening up. He smiled and came over to hug me.

"I can't thank you enough for coming with me to the wedding."

"That's what friends are for," I said, testing him.

"Yeah, right." He struggled with the rusty clanking lock.

"So everything's all right?"

"Just perfect." He swung the door open.

"There's something I need to know…" Just then, Agnes showed up with the other girls. "It can wait." I couldn't risk speaking in front of these gossip-mongers, especially when I was still so unsure of Dumi's intentions.

"Well there's something I need to tell you." He touched the tip of my nose with his index finger. My heart pounded – was he going to say what I thought he would say?

"Trina is coming in at two o'clock today and we're going to do her hair. You and me." It was good news, but I was deflated. There was something more urgent on my mind.

The power went off just after ten. ZESA no longer bothered to warn anyone about their load-shedding schedule, if they had one. A noisy generator was switched on at the house next door. That always happened when the power went off, but you might have thought they would at least have waited until evening. The man who lived there worked for NOCZIM, which explained why he had petrol to burn, but it didn't make it any less of a waste at eleven o'clock in the morning.

"I guess we'll just have to use the solar dryers," I said. Agnes laughed and took some chairs outside. When the power went off we had the clients sit in the sun to dry their hair a little before we styled it.

***

The familiar droning of Trina's diesel engine came up the driveway. She honked and stepped out wearing her trademark khakis. Even with a hairdressing appointment, she still had no sense of style. Dumi grinned and signalled for me to get ready. This would be the first time I'd ever done a white person's hair so I was anxious. He winked at me and I smiled.

"*Makadini Madzimai,*" she said as she offloaded a box from the back of the truck. She paused briefly to glance at the two clients sitting in the sun. "What's going on here?"

"There's no electricity."

"Tell Mrs Khumalo to get a generator."

"Solar is more ecofriendly," Dumi said with a laugh.

She came in and put the box down. Agnes began to check that the supplies were correct. As usual they were and she went to the main house and brought out two boxes of soap. Trina counted them and shook her head, "Five more bars."

"But mum said…"

"Five more bars." Agnes returned and came back with five more bars.

Dumi made a low bow and gestured for Trina to sit in his chair. She handed him plastic bag full of products that I hadn't seen before. Dumi rubbed his hands together and blew on them.

"I'm not too sure about this." Trina seemed to be gritting her teeth.

"It's too late to turn back now, darling," Dumi replied.

He asked me to pin most of her hair up, leaving a little layer at the back of the head. Then he took a tail comb and wove it in and out of the strands, and lifting a section, he placed a foil underneath it, painting the strand with blonde highlighter. He told me to fold the foil over the strand to secure it. With quite an air, he asked me to repeat the process, occasionally making a little correction, until her whole head was covered in foil. It was easier than I thought it would be and I couldn't help standing arms akimbo as every one in the salon looked at our foiled handiwork.

"When you're finished, I'll tell you which one is the 'Hairdresser of Harare'," Trina smiled.

"I'm afraid you're going to have to go solar for half an hour before we do the styling," Dumi said, leading Trina to join the ladies in the sun. "You can work on your tan while you're there."

"Look at these freckles, I'm browner than you are."

Trina sat out in the sun having a conversation about whether the rains would come or not with the other ladies outside. It seems everyone was a farmer to some degree. There was a general consensus that the rainfall patterns had become a lot less predictable. Trina made some mention about a new strain of drought-resistant maize that had been produced by Seedco, and argued that it was dangerous for corporations to patent seed. The other ladies didn't seem to understand this part of the argument, nevertheless they agreed with what she was saying.

The day was going well until a black Mercedes pulled up in the driveway. I did not recall seeing her name on the appointment book but was pleased to see that Minister M___ had brought her husband with her. The chauffeur opened the door and she stepped out wearing a black version of the Robert Mugabe dress she had worn previously. Her braids were coming undone and so she'd come in to get her hair done again.

"*Pamberi neZanu!*" She waved a fist in the air. I was taken aback, she'd never chanted slogans before. When no one responded she shouted, "*Ndati, Pamberi neZanu PF!*'

"*Pamberi NeZanu.*" We replied with limp fists in the air.

"That's much better now. If I'd known that this salon catered for Rhodesians, I would have closed it down a long time ago. Zimbabwe will never be a colony again. How are you Mrs Price? It is good to see you after such a long time."

Trina clenched and unclenched her fists. Her face was a tight mask. She stood up.

"The tobacco you planted before you left did really well. I congratulate you on how well you trained your workers," Minister M___ went on. "Rest assured Good Hope farm is very productive,"

"You already have eight farms, how many more do you need?"

"You should have told that to your ancestors when they were stealing our land. Tell all your friends that we're going to take all the land back and then we're coming for the houses you bought in the suburbs with your ill-gotten riches. *Mabhunu muchapera.*"

"You can't intimidate me. And let me tell you one thing, this tyranny that you call a government is going to collapse when the masses rise up against you."

"If you think your MDC puppets are going to take over this country then you can just forget it…"

Dumi stepped in between the two women.

"This is my place of business. There will be no politics here."

Minister M___'s husband was standing on the sidelines; his eyes drooped as though he had no interest in the exchange. His roughly shaven face told the story of a man who'd seen a lot in the world and of life.

"Go back to Britain you white pig."

"I'm not going anywhere. This is my home and I have as much right as you to be here."

"Minister M___ if you persist in insulting other clients I shall have to ask you to leave." Dumi spoke firmly, holding out his hand for Trina to stop talking. Mr M___ raised his eyebrows and stroked his chin.

The way in which Dumisani conducted himself took the minister aback. She blinked, unused to being spoken to in this way, and then quickly regained her composure.

"Young man, if the MDC is teaching you to be a dog to white people then I shall teach you a lesson you will never forget."

"This is not about the MDC, it is not about Black or White or any other kind of division. I'm telling you to respect our other clients who are here."

"Mrs Khumalo will be firing you very soon."

"That's fine by me, madam, but as it stands this is my salon. Now if you want your hair done go inside, if not goodbye and have a nice day."

Minister M___ walked inside in a huff and her husband followed her slowly with his hands in his pockets. Trina had turned red and was breathing heavily as if she was about to cry. The minister reached for her phone and made a call. I didn't catch all of it but I heard her say, "Tell the war vets to come to Khumalo's salon in the Avenues."

"It's no longer safe for you here. You must leave," Dumi said to Trina.

"I'm not going anywhere. I know my rights."

"I can do your hair at your place or anywhere else you choose, but not here."

Trina stood her ground and insisted that she was not leaving until she was finished. The minister asked me to do her hair saying how much she regretted having a sell-out do it on the previous occasion. I started undoing the braids and prayed that Trina would see sense and leave, for all our sakes.

"I'm not going anywhere."

"Then you leave me with no choice... but to try and defend you as best I can." Dumi bowed his head and stayed beside her. He bounced up and down on the balls of his feet like a rugby player waiting for the whistle to blow. I wanted to tell him not to be stupid, but I dared not utter a word. After what seemed to be an eternity of waiting, Trina finally said, "All right, I'll leave."

There was a collective sight of relief. My hands trembled as I undid the minister's hair. There was just one problem. The minister's Merc was blocking the driveway.

"Can you move your car out of my way?" Trina asked, her voice tightly controlled. I felt sorry for her with her hair packed into its shiny silver sheaths. No matter who or when they were removed, her hair was bound to dry or burn, and the colour would be something else. What was supposed to be a treat had turned into a nightmare.

"You're not going anywhere until the war vets get here," the minister shouted.

Trina repeated her plea, this time to the chauffeur who was standing jiggling his keys. He did not budge an inch. She repeated herself but the man laughed in her face. The clock was ticking, the war vets were coming.

"Tawanda, move your car out of Mrs Price's way." Mr M___ spoke in a gentle authoritative voice.

"Don't even think about it Tawanda!" the minister responded.

"*Iwe. Usakanganwe kuti murume ndiyani panapa,*" Mr M___ said pointing a finger at her. She kept quiet and Tawanda went to do as requested.

It was a relief to see Trina leave, because two minutes later a pick-up packed with men carrying knobkerries arrived. A dozen of them clambered down singing revolutionary songs. Most of them seemed younger than I was. As they came toward the salon Minister M___ called out to them, "That boy is a member of the MDC."

Twenty-three

The armed war vets approached whistling and chanting. I dropped the comb I was using to unbraid the minister and covered my mouth. The mental image of Dumi beaten to a pulp, sprawled on the ground, flashed though my mind. The mob circled him. It was like watching a hunting party waiting to make a move. Dumi turned and looked at all of them, then he put his hands behind his back staring forward into space defiantly. I wanted him to beg for mercy. I wanted to plead with Minister M___ but my voice abandoned me. There were pains in my abdomen I could not explain. Standing in the middle of this ring of death, Dumi was calm looking like a lion amongst jackals.

"What are you waiting for?" he said.

One of them raised his knobkerrie. Dumi took a deep breath.

"That's enough!" Mr M___ walked into the circle and instructed the war vets to get back into their vehicle. I wanted to rush forward and kiss him on his stubbly chin. Minister M___ was shaking with rage beneath me as Mr M___ put his hand around Dumi's shoulders in an affectionate fatherly gesture.

The other girls in the salon looked at each other. Their faces relaxed with relief while the remaining clients were still frozen in their seats. The war vets drove off singing revolutionary songs, victors of the third Chimurenga.

"You're a very brave young man. We could have used you during the liberation struggle," said Mr M___, his hand still thrown around Dumi's shoulders. I did not hear Dumi's reply but it must have been thank you.

Mr M___ had run away from school to join the war against colonial oppression. He had distinguished himself on many occasions and was known to have been one of the fiercest commanders operating in the north of the country. When the war was over, he joined the newly formed Zimbabwe National Army and had served until 1987 when he left to form his own businesses. I realised that what I liked most about him was a sense of peace and of dignity that I reckoned was the product of him having seen too much suffering. It was, however, the first time that I'd seen him overrule his wife. Usually he was content to hang about with a disinterested air.

The two of them moved out of earshot, talking. I was grateful that nothing had happened to my Dumisani.

***

We went to the cinema that night. It was strange, because I now associated movie houses with church. The film we chose was *Hitch*, in the hope of seeing Will Smith's fine rippling body. Dumi said that he appreciated his versatility, how he had moved from rap and comedy to becoming an award-winning movie actor. I just wanted to see those cute ears. We bought some pop-corn and sipped on Coca-Cola. The last time I'd been to the cinema was with Phillip. It had been a very different experience. He'd kept talking about how much money he was making, as though that was all that life was about. Then I'd listened keenly, but now I looked back in disgust.

"Next time we'll have to come and see something that's PG rated so we can bring Chiwoniso with us," Dumi said casually, not knowing how much it meant to me that he thought about my daughter.

The lights in the cinema dimmed and the movie started. Dumi's hand slid across the divider to hold mine. There was a man at the bottom of the room with a terrible cough. Every two minutes, he coughed, spluttered and wheezed so we couldn't hear. The parts of the film we did hear were hilarious, the dialogue between Will Smith and Eva Mendes more so. There was a collective 'ahh' when the movie ended. We remained in our seats until the last person had left.

We left satisfied. I told him I was afraid that he could have been killed by the war vets, but he laughed the incident off as if it had been a very minor thing. I told him how close he had come to death or at least being wounded but my words didn't seem to register.

"Those men were cowards. It is through fear that they manipulate people. Do you know the story of the owl's horns?"

"I've never heard it."

"A long time ago, before the time of men, when animals and birds ruled the world, the birds saw that animals had the lion as their king and decided to choose one for themselves. The owl insisted that because he alone had horns, he should be the ruler. They were so afraid of his terrible horns that in the end they never chose a king for themselves. And so it was that the owl ruled through fear until one day when he was asleep as usual during the day, a little sparrow checked the 'terrible horns' and discovered that they were in fact overgrown ears."

"Not everyone's as brave as you are."

"That's because we've forgotten who we are. We are the sons of Dombo and the Rozvis. We are the children of the builders of the Great Zimbabwe, the eternal city of stone. Why have the children of the great Mzilikazi become cowards? How can the sons of Munhumutapa tremble before any man?" I'd never seen this side of him before: the passion, the strength, the determination.

We walked hand in hand through the city. We passed beneath broken streetlights and I felt as if there were only the two of us in the whole universe, with a crescent moon above. Dumi put his arm around me and we walked along like lovers. On the way we passed drunkards pissing in corners and prostitutes flashing for business.

"Do you mind walking home?"

"It's a beautiful night," I said, not wanting it to end.

***

The sight of Mrs Khumalo behind the cash desk greeted us on Wednesday morning. She was still in her nightdress and had a frown on her face. We greeted her but she did not reply, sipping a cup of tea silently and resting her chin on her knuckles.

"I know you want to talk about what happened yesterday," Dumi said finally.

"You have no idea the number of problems you have caused me."

"She was way out of order..."

"That is not the way you deal with these people. It only makes things worse."

"Trina is your supplier and your friend. I could not stand aside whilst she was abused. The same goes for all our clients."

"Listen!" Mrs Khumalo banged her fist on the table. "I don't care what you think or what your principles are. You do not do what you did yesterday. Never ever do it again. Do I make myself clear... I said, 'do I make myself clear?'"

Dumi nodded and I did the same, as if I'd been involved. The chair scraped back as Mrs Khumalo stood up. She walked warily to the door. "I forgot to tell you one more thing. We're closing shop for two weeks starting on Sunday. This will give us time to do those renovations we spoke of earlier. It will also give us time for things to cool down."

We told Yolanda and Memory about the two-week break and they seemed relieved to hear it. Charlie Boy kept saying that Dumi was either very brave or mad.

"I'm just mad," Dumi replied.

I tried to phone Trina but she did not answer. I left a voicemail on her phone saying we just needed to know if she was okay. There was a chance she would never come back. I certainly wouldn't do so if what had happened to her had happened to me. She was our friend, but part of me wondered whether it was good for her or us if she returned. Yolanda suggested that Agnes could pick up the supplies from her place instead. The thought of changing a supplier would have been insupportable to Mrs Khumalo. There was no one else in the city who did what Trina did with the same level of integrity.

The kid selling freezits came over but we shooed him away. No one was in the mood. We worked as we usually did but our spirits were low. I noticed how we all kept locking out the widow as if fear-

ful that a truckload of war vets would arrive, and any time a client's
car pulled up, my heart skipped a beat.

The day dragged. Clients spoke about the usual stuff: work, family, economic problems, husband trouble and the like, but none of us
seemed interested. It was as though part of our vitality, our life force,
had been sucked out by some invisible agent. The urban grooves on
the radio did nothing to improve my disposition. Dumi mimed along
but his mind was elsewhere, I was sure of it.

Then I saw a slight smile on his face – the private smile of someone in love.

Twenty-four

The weekend came and went and it was a relief to know that we were going to be away from the salon for a while. Nonetheless, I woke up early on Monday morning as usual. Habits born through years of work cannot be easily set aside. I drank my tea and took a walk through the garden. Fungai had done a marvellous job with the flowers. He had watered the grass and it had left its dry yellow behind and was beginning to turn green, and he'd removed all the weeds. If only the weeds from my past could be removed just as easily.

I stood at the gate and looked at the long procession of Churchill boys and Roosevelt girls going to school. Was there a future for them when they finished, I wondered? The generations who came before us had stolen hope to such an extent that we regarded the future with trepidation. I knew people who never looked beyond the next day. Their circumstances only allowed them to focus on the here and now, which is pretty much what animals did, though we regarded ourselves as superior.

In the afternoon I went to look for maize meal. There was none at the local shopping centre so I walked up to Rhodesville where I'd heard there might be some available. It was a long walk but the weather was cool. I couldn't find any mealie-meal but bought a kilogram packet of rice and some chicken feet, which is all my finances would allow. I decided I would make peanut butter rice because it was Chiwoniso's favourite. I couldn't remember when we'd last eaten meat so the chicken legs would be a treat; Maidei knew how to prepare them well.

When I returned, Dumi was lounging on the grass reading a magazine. He waved and called out to me.

"What are you doing on Friday night?"

"Nothing at all." I replied.

"My parents would like us to go for dinner and maybe stay the weekend."

"I can do dinner but I can't stay, I have to look after Chiwoniso."

"They want to see her too."

"You mean they know about her?"

"I already told them and they're delighted at the prospect of having a little one run around the house. They haven't got any grand kids yet so she might brighten up their day."

I was shocked. They were happy for their son to be seeing a single mother who happened to be older than him. Most families I know would never contemplate such a match let alone encourage it.

"They don't mind the fact that I have a child?"

"Why should they?"

It was very modern of them but still something didn't feel quite right.

"So what do you say? I have to let them know by tonight."

"I would love to."

***

Friday came and I was a bundle of nerves. Chiwoniso knew we were going to see Uncle Dumi's house and she was excited. She kept running around asking when we would leave. I had never taken her on a holiday or anywhere besides church. There had never been any money for that.

"Let's go, Michelle is waiting at the gate," Dumi said clicking his phone off.

Michelle was driving a blue Mitsubishi twin-cab which seemed far too large for her tiny body. I wondered how she managed to reach the pedals but she seemed to be driving all right.

"It feels wrong when I drive on the left because in America you have to drive on the right."

"You always talk about America, we're tired of it," Dumi said, pretending to be annoyed.

"You're just jealous because you refused to go abroad then and now you want to."

"I have no business going abroad. Everything I want is right here."

"I want to go to America," Chiwoniso shouted. I was fighting to hold her as she was jumping up and down on the seat.

Michelle took no notice of her antics. "Then why do you have a visa to go to the UK in December?" she asked her brother.

"I didn't know that had come through."

"Mum said it came through today. If I were you, I'd have gone somewhere sexy like France or Italy."

"How long will you be gone for?" I asked.

"It should be a six-month visa but I will have to see how much time Mrs Khumalo will give me for my leave."

We passed a traffic accident. A kombi had hit a small passenger car and they were on the roadside waiting for the police to come.

"You really should take Vimbai with you. That's the problem with men, they only think about themselves."

"Maybe she doesn't want to go. It'll be winter there, after all."

"I don't have a passport."

Michelle slammed the brakes on and pulled over to the side of the road. The cars behind us hooted angrily.

"How the hell can you live without a passport?" She seemed genuinely pissed off. I wanted to apologise.

"Hey, it's none of your business whether she has one or not."

"Shut up Dumi, this is between me and my *muroora*. Vimbai darling, we have to go to the passport office first thing Monday morning and get you pimped out."

I wanted to say that I didn't have money to even think about going abroad but the determined look on Michelle's face made me mutter a half-hearted agreement. Only then did she put the car into gear and drive back onto the road.

When we arrived a maid came out to collect our bags. She went to put them in our room.

"Mum and dad are at the Chanakiras. They'll be back in time for dinner." Luke came over to greet me with a kiss on the cheeks. "This must be Chiwoniso. I know the old folks are really looking forward to seeing her. Don't be nervous, my girlfriend Sandra is meant to be here any time soon. You'll love her, she's really nice, like everyone in the family. Be careful of Michelle though, she wants you all to herself."

Luke was slightly taller than Dumi and had piercing eyes. He had the same athletic build that seemed to run in the family's male DNA. I later learnt that he had played tennis for Zimbabwe at junior level. We sat in the lounge in front of a massive wide-screen TV. It was tuned to MTV and we watched the videos of rappers and gyrating girls coming on screen at three-minute intervals. Michelle offered a running commentary on who had won what rap battle; who was hot and who was not; and who had a beef with whom. If there was anything American then she had a running commentary to go with it. Chiwoniso stuck to her side, fascinated by this new 'auntie' who had a strange accent.

Sandra came in and apologised for her lateness. She was a coloured girl with green eyes and long frizzy hair. She offered me a limp hand and regarded me with barely concealed contempt as if asking: 'what is this township girl doing here?' Her pearly white teeth flashed at me in the brief imitation of a smile. She moved over to Luke and curled round him like a python on its prey.

Mr and Mrs Ncube came in soon afterwards and we were herded into the dining room, which was very spacious with a mahogany table that could seat twelve. The maids brought in mountains of food – more than we could hope to finish. There was rice, roast duck, beef, vegetables, mushroom soup and four other side-dishes which I could not identify.

"I hope you like the food," Mrs Ncube said to me sounding a little nervous after she had said grace.

"It looks lovely," I replied.

"Only the best for the girl who cured my son."

"Come on let's get stuck in," Mr Ncube said rather abruptly. Dumi, sitting beside his father, maintained a somewhat stony expression. Avoiding looking at anyone else, he kept his eyes on his plate. There was the slightest of tremors in his hands as he picked up his fork.

I'd never eaten duck before, but I had a far greater problem: like my daughter sitting next to me, I had limited experience of using a knife and fork. The only period when I had used them was with Phillip, and that was a long time ago. I struggled with the fork in my left hand and spilt my rice onto my lap. I could feel them looking at me and didn't know what to do. The more I tried the more food I dropped. Mr Ncube put down his fork and knife and picked up a spoon. When he began to eat with it everyone, except for Sandra, did the same. She carried on with her knife and fork. Mr Ncube winked at me, seeing I was relieved to be eating with the right hand. It seems they were making every effort to ensure I was comfortable. The food was delicious, very different from anything I had ever eaten before. This was the sort of thing people only ate in fine hotels. I made the resolution to learn to use a fork to save myself from future embarrassment.

Twenty-five

The bed my daughter and I slept in had satin sheets that caressed the skin. Chiwoniso kept sliding down them, excited by the smooth luxuriant comfort. There was a large window from which we could see the stars as they shone brightly in the sky. This must be what heaven was like. I rubbed my full tummy and thought about where my life was headed. Still I had not asked Dumi what his true intentions were. I was afraid that he would turn around and say this was just some sort of practical joke. I also wondered what his mother meant when she said that I had cured him. Perhaps he had suffered a broken heart that I knew nothing about. It took me a long time to fall sleep.

I was woken early in the morning by the sound of birds. The rest of the family were still asleep so I made my way downstairs. A maid was already cleaning. She must have started at six in the morning or thereabouts.

"*Mangwanani.*" She greeted me with a heart-warming smile and asked if I would like some coffee. I asked for tea instead.

"What time do the family wake up?"

"On Saturdays around ten in the morning, sometimes later." Her voice sounded rural so I asked where she was from. She told me that she was from Muzarabani and she had been brought here to work.

The country girls made better maids, because as they had no family and friends in the city, they would be tied to the house with a lower risk that they could get pregnant or run away. With a little twist of fate, I could have been the person working here, but now I was the one sleeping between satin sheets. I was not surprised to discover she earned no more than my own house-girl who received the minimum gazetted by law.

"Would you like me to bath your daughter when she wakes up?"

"Please do."

I went out and stood by the pool. It felt as if my life was rising with the sun. My shadow fell onto the water and I inhaled the morning air. If this is how the other one-thousandth lived then I wanted to be one of them. Fate was smiling down on me for a change.

***

We had breakfast by the pool. Bacon, eggs, beans and toast, a whole other meal again. The shortages obviously did not mean anything to the Ncubes. Chiwoniso was a picture of joy. She latched on to Mr Ncube who was only happy to play the role of the genial step-grand-father. She tickled his moustache and he roared with laughter. Everyone wanted a piece of her except for Sandra, who did not have a maternal bone in her body. Children have some form of innate intuition and Chiwoniso stayed right away from her.

"How're things at the salon?" Mrs Ncube asked.

"They're not too bad… "

"I wasn't asking you, I was asking my *muroora*."

"It's like I don't exist anymore," Dumi said with a little chortle.

"It is just great. Once the renovations are done it will be much better. Perhaps you'll come there to get your hair done."

"I already have my hairdresser who I have gone to for the last twenty years. Maybe if you started your own salon I might be tempted to change."

"That's my dream."

"Then what's stopping you?" asked Mr Ncube.

"It's expensive to get the equipment and the products to get started. I'll get there one day maybe not today or tomorrow, but I will."

"That's the spirit. You all see that? That's the sort of determination this country needs. I'm not too different from you, my girl." He waved a finger in the air to emphasise his point. "I was born and raised in Zvimba. I went to Kutama mission. My parents were so poor that I didn't have shoes to wear. To pay my way through school I worked for the missionaries in their gardens in the afternoons and during the holidays; when others were playing I was working. At the time I hated it but it gave me a good work ethic unlike the people you see today all wanting to make a quick buck without doing a stroke of real work.

"After school I came to Harare to look for work; I got a job as a messenger for Johnsons on Union Avenue. Those days those were the only jobs blacks could do. It was tough to advance myself, I had my parents and brothers to look after back home but I told myself that I was going to go forward in life. I was going to be somebody. Let me tell you, some of my friends who I went to work with are still doing menial jobs, but not me. I saved what little money I could so that I could start something of my own. I bought a Renault. Do you remember those cars? It was a fine little car back then. They don't make them like that anymore. I began to go to South Africa and come back with radios and TVs that I sold at a profit. From there I opened a small liquor store in Mufakose and then another one in Mabvuku. I was always on the lookout for the next opportunity. You have to keep your ear to the ground, feel the pulse of the nation, know the right people to talk to. I expanded, building shops in rural growth points where no one else wanted to invest. Then, for a brief period, I moved into shipping. That was a disaster. I got out quickly. I was one of the first people to put commuter omnibuses on the road, the South Africans had them decades before us and I saw that was the future, Zupco was breaking down and people needed cover. Now I have properties: three gold mines, shops, buses, brick manufacturing companies, shares in all the major banks and cellphone companies in the country and I'm still always looking out for the next investment opportunity. It's a difficult world, but if you are determined to succeed no one can stop you. Look at my kids, they were born with silver spoons in their mouths and they're all waiting for me to die so they can destroy my wealth. Well, let me tell you something: there are only two men in this country who will never die, and I'm one of them."

I discovered that this was a speech he made at every family gathering. It omitted the numerous palms he'd greased along the way to get himself lucrative government contracts. But it did nothing to diminish the fact that he was a self-made man who had risen from being a barefooted villager to being one of the wealthiest men in the country. The diversity of his investments was astounding in itself. The two eldest boys worked in the family business but Dumi had so far refused to be involved. This was a cause for disappointment. I reflected that the possibility of other disadvantaged boys being able to advance themselves in a similar manner was now virtually impossible given the situation the country was in.

***

We drove for a family day out to a game park in Hwedza. It was set in beautiful savannah land with trees everywhere. Monkeys leapt from tree to tree welcoming us, leering into the car, hoping for food, but there were signs everywhere telling us not to feed the monkeys. The car bumped along the gravel road and Michelle took photos. There were giraffes browsing from the tops of small trees, duikers bounded across the road while elephants lumbered slowly along with their young in tow. The animals mingled at the watering hole, safe and protected from poachers. The sheer beauty of the scenery made me wish I had a home in the country.

We reached the main site where the managers had thatched lodges for paying guests. Smiling staff in green uniforms brought us refreshments to quench our throats.

"They have black rhinos here too. There are very few of them left in the world," Dumi told Chiwoniso.

"Our teacher taught us to draw a rhino."

"I have a special treat just for you." Her eyes lit up and she clasped her hands in anticipation. He led her by the hand to a waiting ranger who took her toward an enclosure where they had a baby black rhino.

"This is our newest baby rhino. Her name is Tsitsi," the ranger said.

"Tsitsi," Chiwoniso repeated stroking the little rhino's ears.

Twenty-six

The queue at the passport office was the longest I'd ever encountered, which was saying something. It stretched right round the Registrar's office and onto the street. All the people waiting in line seemed to be young. Their desperation to leave the country showed on their faces. A thin security guard whose blue overalls hung on his matchstick frame walked around with a baton stick ordering people to stay in their places. It was ironic that during the war of independence people had not left in the way they were doing now under the same revolutionary government that had freed them. Could it really be that independence had become a greater burden than the yoke of colonial oppression?

Street kids stood in the queue as well. They were an enterprising lot, selling their places towards the front and then promptly rejoining the queue at the back and waiting for the next impatient soul to buy their place. Queuing was now such an ingrained part of the economy that the prices they charged were fairly uniform, as if there was some sort of regulatory authority. The invisible hand of economics was at work.

"Don't worry, we won't have to stay for long. I hate bloody queues," Michelle said as she dialled a number on her phone. She spoke with someone briefly and hung up. "Let's go wait at the front."

We waited for half an hour and then a man in a white shirt and yellow tie came to get us. He took us to his office and shut the door. It was a room full of dusty old files that had not been opened for ages. There was nothing on his desk except for the day's newspaper and a pen. It was clear that productive work seldom took place at this table.

"What can I do for you today, *mainini* Michelle?" There was a familiarity between them that told me he had done this before.

"My *muroora* here needs to get a passport asap."

"These things are more difficult now than they used to be. There are more people to feed in the food chain."

"Will this be enough?" She placed two bricklike wads of money on the table and slid them to him. He swiftly grabbed them and put them in a drawer under his desk.

"Stay here. I'll be right back."

Another half hour passed and the man returned with some forms, apologising profusely that he had been delayed by a small emergency. I filled out the form and had my fingerprints taken. It was sent off together with two passport photos that I'd brought with me at Michelle's insistence. Within a month I would get my first ever passport. When we left, the queue had barely moved because people like us had kept jumping to the front.

‡

When we returned to the Ncube home, Dumi was pacing about the carport. He seemed relieved to see us.

"You told me you would be back by twelve."

"There's no need to panic. You guys have plenty of time," Michelle replied.

"Time for what?" I asked.

"Get in and pack your bags. Leave Chiwoniso's things, it's a surprise my parents arranged for us. If we're not already too late."

In no time we were back in the car and on the road. They refused to tell me where we were going. It was only after we had driven through Hatfield that I knew we were on the airport road. My heart thumped. I looked up at the street lights – the only ones working in Harare – and realised that every one of them had a poster of the president attached to it. His face was everywhere looking down at us.

"We're off to Victoria Falls." Dumi's voice was high-pitched with excitement.

"But I don't have a passport yet."

"It's a domestic flight, you won't need one."

Michelle dropped us off and gave us both big hugs.

"Don't do anything I wouldn't do," she shouted to us as we disappeared through the doors.

I was sick as our small aircraft bounced up and down in turbulence. There were only half a dozen other people with us, white tourists. The rows of empty seats punctuated an absence that I was to witness more of. Dumi was his usual relaxed self, holding my hand while struggling not to doze off. I looked out of the window and saw how small everything down below had become.

"My parents must really like you."

"Your family is really nice."

"You see that guy over there with the white hair. I've seen him on TV. He must be a BBC journalist sneaking in."

The man with the white hair cast an anxious glance at us. Dumi waved at him and he turned away.

"They're always creeping in. I sometimes watch their reports and they have nothing new to say but they speak in low whispers as if they are afraid of something, as if they are reporting from a war zone when the worst thing that could happen to them is a hasty deportation."

We took a taxi from the little airport in Victoria Falls to Kingdom Hotel. It was the nearest to the falls, situated right inside the national park. We could hear the roar of the water in the distance. The hotel's stone architecture was based on that of Great Zimbabwe, but its thatched roofs reminded me of the Ncube's residence. We checked in and a bored porter took our bags and led us to our room. I panicked when I saw the room only had one double bed. When Dumi unpacked his bag I realised we were sharing the room. He looked so casual, as if bringing a woman to a hotel room was nothing new to him. What sort of parents booked their son into a hotel with a woman he was not married to? Did they think I was a prostitute or something?

"Are you all right? You look tense."

"I'm just fine," I snapped.

"The day is still young. I was thinking we could hang around the hotel and then maybe go and see the falls tomorrow."

I shrugged my shoulders. He was not going to get into my pants this easily. I may be a woman with a child born out of wedlock but that didn't mean I had no morals. This was not the first time in my life I'd been seduced by a rich man. I hoped Dumi was different. I couldn't bear to live through everything I'd suffered with Phillip all over again.

We spent the whole afternoon by the swimming pool where Dumi made an attempt to teach me to swim. We were the only ones there, the place was deserted. In the evening we went to the casino. A handful of foreign tourists played blackjack. We sat alone at the roulette table and Dumi explained the rules to me. Evens, odds, red, black, I couldn't understand it despite his best attempts. We gambled slowly, losing slowly.

"So you're a man who likes international news?" The white-haired man from the plane appeared from behind us and placed a friendly arm on Dumi's shoulder.

"When it's about Zimbabwe it's domestic to me," Dumi replied and offered his hand to the journalist who shook it.

"Quite right, I forget that sometimes. It comes from having worked in too many countries. Half the time I don't know where the hell I am. Anyway since you've recognised me, there's no need for me to introduce myself." He gave a weary smile and winked at me. "What can I get you and this beautiful goddess? Waitress, can you please bring the drinks menu for me and my friends."

"What have you come to report about this time?"

"Just a piece about the collapsing tourism industry, that's all. I mean look at this fine hotel. Friendly staff, great rooms, it easily competes with the finest in the world but there is hardly anyone here."

"So you'll do a piece that will scare even more people away. I can't see how that can help things. Why don't you wait for an election? That's when things get really interesting."

"It's such a shame though. If what was happening here was happening in any other country in the world, there would have been a civil war by now."

"That's the last thing we need."

"The people here don't have the stomach for it. The last time I was here, I was on the road to a little town called Chin-hoyeee, do you know it? It's sort of on your way to Kariba, in the west. Anyway, I had a puncture. Now, I haven't a clue how to change a tyre but this ancient Land Rover just pulls up beside me and this guy who was travelling with his family and chickens asks if I'm okay and just goes on to change the damn tyre for me. I didn't even need to ask him to do it. If it wasn't for him, I'd still be stuck there today. So I'm there thinking I need to pay him a little something but instead he thrusts this chicken at me. It's quacking and having a go at me with its beak; I tried saying no but he insisted. I didn't want to offend him so I took it. I had to spend the rest of my trip with this chicken flapping about in the back of the car." He flapped his arms as some sort of imitation and laughed with us.

The waitress brought our drinks and placed them on the table.

"A story like that doesn't make for great news."

"Yeah, but it makes for great memories." There was a glint in the journalist's eye. "So what do you do, anyway?"

"We're hairdressers," I chipped in.

The journalist ran his hand through his thinning hair.

"I'm afraid there's nothing we can do for you up there," Dumi said with a cheeky laugh.

When the journalist heard that Dumi was taking a trip to England, he offered him his phone number and told him, "Come and see me any time." The two of them spent most of the evening chatting non-stop while I was content to lose money on the table. This was another thing about Dumi, he had a hunger to speak with people wherever he was, about anything at all. It was as if he felt the need to connect with everyone he came across. By the time we went to bed, I was slightly tipsy

***

We got to our room and Dumisani began to undress. I got between the sheets fully clothed. When he saw I was nervous Dumi took the cover and a few pillows and made himself a bed on the floor. I tried to sleep but could not bear the thought of him lying on the hard floor.

"Come into bed," I said to him

"Are you sure? If I'd known you would be uncomfortable sharing a room, I would've asked my parents to get us separate rooms."

"It's not fair for you to sleep on that hard floor."

He got up, grateful that he didn't have to, and lay beside me. I had to tell him what had happened to me in the past – a secret that I had carried with me for a very long time. I figured that if there was anyone I could tell it to, it was Dumi.

I spoke very slowly because it is hard to let words out that you have kept in a safe for so long: "Phillip raped me. ... That's how I got pregnant with Chiwoniso. ... What's wrong with men? I stayed with him because I loved him despite the fact that he hurt me. I thought maybe it was my fault for not doing what he wanted in the first place... " I could not speak anymore.

"It's not your fault. I'm here to protect you now." I felt him tremble with emotion as he held me close, as if he wanted to take the pain away. He held me the whole night and never let go. I had never felt safer in a man's arms

In the morning we took a stroll down to the falls. I felt a spiritual renewal and joy that I didn't know existed. We passed through the rain forest – was it the only forest in the world that was sustained by spray? We felt it all over our bodies as we walked, delicious and cooling at first, and then I realised that we were going to get very wet, as if we'd been drenched in a storm. What the hell, I thought, we'll dry off. Dumi pointed out various species of plants that were found nowhere else in the country. The roar of the water grew louder with each step we took.

"The correct name for it is Mosi-oa-Tunya, the smoke that thunders." Dumi enjoyed playing the role of tour guide. "The whites even tried to claim that David Livingstone discovered it because the locals were too afraid to come near it. It's strange how they also include the fact that the locals showed it to him. That's a paradox only a colonial mind can maintain."

The falls appeared before us in all their glory. Water cascaded down the gorge and sprayed up with the might of God's power. There are many of us who've died without seeing this wonder of wonders in our own country. A rainbow arched across the waterfalls as surely as it had done since the day Noah's ark set down on dry land.

"If the water falls and there are no tourists to hear it, does it make a sound?" Dumi asked.

I laughed.

Twenty-seven

Mrs Khumalo had outdone herself. The new salon building was completed on schedule. The front wall had been knocked down and replaced by a glass front with large sliding doors. Charlie Boy's barbershop now had its own separate glass partition. He began to say 'step into my office' to each client who came in to see him. The walls were painted glossy white and she had mirrors placed all round the room. Of course the posters remained but I was happy to see that the condom adverts had now been relegated to the cash desk. The exterior had been painted pink with a new neon sign that worked when we had electricity.

On the management side, Dumi excelled and I saw why Mrs Khumalo had picked him. He brought in extra staff and created a rota so that we didn't have to work seven days a week. I never got to meet the new girls he hired because of my schedule but I heard they were as good as the rest of us. Even Agnes seemed more amiable at times. It was as if a new wave of optimism had struck us and we'd become like one big happy family. Mrs Khumalo even spoke of opening a new branch somewhere in the city centre. Perhaps I would be manager there if that happened.

The planets had converged and I felt happy. I went into work with a smile and left with an even bigger smile. At home I was happier too. I would get up in the morning and see Dumi at the breakfast table with Chiwoniso. We now worked different shifts because of the new rota and so we only ever worked three shifts out of five together. In the evenings Dumi would help her with her homework while I watched soaps on TV.

"I wish I could introduce you to my parents," I said to him one night when we were alone in the lounge.

"Give it time. These things have a way of sorting themselves out. The family will want you back again once bruised egos heal."

"They're really nice people. It's just this one issue we can't seem to get around. I want to introduce you to my brother Fungai though."

"The mad philosopher."

"Don't call him that." Even though it had been said in jest I found myself slightly annoyed.

Dumi rubbed my arm and apologised. He knew how protective I had become of the one family member who still spoke to me. I lay my head on his shoulder and smelt the cologne on him, a scent that lingered. He yawned and rubbed his eyes.

"Feeling sleepy?"

"Just a little. You're lucky you don't have to go to work tomorrow."

"Poor thing."

"I have half a mind to change the rota so you go instead of me."

***

That night I lay in bed unable to sleep. A yearning that I had not felt for a long time returned to me. I felt whole like a woman again. I went to the bathroom and washed my face then changed into my red nightdress with thin straps that made me look curvy. There was a small part of my mind telling me that this was the right thing to do. Tonight was the night.

I walked barefoot and stood outside the door to Dumi's room. I took a deep breath and willed myself to knock but I couldn't. My hand was raised but it refused to go any further. What if he was fast asleep? I stood like that for an eternity before I had the courage to knock lightly three times.

"Come in." Dumi did not sound drowsy.

I walked in and stood at the foot of the bed. Dumi looked at me, his eyes quickly devoured my body before he turned them modestly away. I felt a slight tremor pass through me and then I crawled onto the bed moving up until I straddled him. I could feel him shaking beneath me. Was it passion or was I seeing him unnerved for the first time?

"Hello," he said, in a timid voice much like a mouse squeak.

"Hello." My own voice was slightly hoarse. I caressed his chest and began to kiss his abs. His perfect torso shivered with every touch. I ran my tongue over his belly button and slowly moved up to his chest. I could feel his heart pounding beneath me. His skin was soft but his muscles were rock solid. I kissed his neck and could feel a slight stubble. His hands lay flaccid beside him as if he did not know what to do. I took them and guided him towards me. My breathing grew louder and louder. I could hear it in my ears. There was a fire burning through me, which I'd never felt for any man before.

But Dumi tensed when I kissed his lips.

"Are you okay?"

"Yeah."

"Kiss me, don't be scared."

We kissed and his lips felt tender. I was aching for him, desperate to have him make love to me. When I tried to pull his pants off, he said, "Stop."

"What's the matter?"

"We mustn't." Was he teasing me?

"It's all right." I kissed him.

"We can't do this."

"Don't you trust me?"

"It's not that."

"Then tell me what it is."

Maybe he didn't find me attractive. He hadn't given me that impression. Had I moved too quickly? What if he thought I was a whore? Thoughts ran through my mind. I needed to understand why he was rejecting me.

"I really like you, but I think we should wait. One day we will get married and I want everything to be perfect. I've never slept with a woman. It's old-fashioned I guess but it is the right way to do things."

That night I lay in his arms with my mind swirling. Dumi was a rare find, a man for whom sex was not the only thing. I could hardly believe it. A man as attractive as Dumi, with all his connections and opportunities, a virile young man of twenty-two... I closed my eyes remembering how he had mentioned marriage. I knew I'd waited my whole life to find someone I could give myself to, so it didn't matter if I had to wait just a little longer.

***

When I woke up, Dumi had snuck off to work. I imagine he must have planted a kiss on my cheek before he left. Maidei gave me a suggestive look when I left his room that morning. One woman to another saying, 'You got lucky'. I sort of had in a way. I ate my breakfast and sat down to watch another boring talk-show on morning TV. Maidei swept the house stealing glances at me whenever she could. I felt happy.

A car pulled up outside the gate and hooted. I sent Maidei to see who it was. She came back running. It was Phillip. I sent her back to tell him to go away. She soon returned saying that he insisted he needed to speak with me. The idea of using my house-girl as a go-between did not appeal to me, so I put on my morning gown and went down to the gate.

"Have you come to break more windows?" I said in the most hostile voice I could muster.

"Hi Vimbai. I came to see you. I needed to apologise about what happened at the wedding. I was out of order." His voice was low and sounded awkward because he was trying his best not show his still missing teeth. I wondered why on earth he had not got them fixed. He could afford to.

"You've made your apology now go away."

"I brought you some groceries." It had been a long time since he had done that for me.

"I don't need your groceries or anything else from you."

"There are toys in there that I bought for Chiwoniso. Please at least accept these for her sake."

"You gave up your responsibilities towards your daughter a long time ago. We need nothing from you. If this was all you wanted then I think it is time for you to leave."

"You have never spoken to me like this before." His voice registered shock, which quickly turned to menace. "That boy you're seeing, does he know whose daughter Chiwoniso is?"

"I don't keep dirty secrets like you. He knows and he also knows what you did to me. If you ever come back here again you will lose the rest of your teeth. I hope I am making my self clear."

I left him there by the gate. He lingered for a while and drove off. Coming to terms with my past was more empowering than I'd ever imagined it could be.

Twenty-eight

The day before my birthday, six months after Dumi had first walked into my life, I worked a half-day and he had arranged a day off for both of us the following day so we could celebrate as a family. Yolanda gave me a card she had made herself. For a moment, I wished I was her age again, carefree and in the prime of youth – though, come to think of it, when had I ever been carefree? When had any young people with my background?

The months had rolled by in easy succession. Dumi was thoroughly domesticated and spent most of his days with Chiwoniso and me. It was nice to have the house to myself when, once a fortnight or so, he would vanish to do his own thing. On such days, the first thing he did when he came back would be hunt around the house until he found Chiwoniso and give her a treat. Come December, Dumi would be off to the UK for his holidays. I had my passport but no desire to go with him since Mrs Ncube had tempted me with the offer to join the family over Christmas.

A familiar Benz pulled up the driveway but it was not the minister who was in it but her husband, who entered the salon looking very unsure of himself. He'd left the engine running and kept glancing back at the car as if to comfort himself that he could make a quick getaway if needs be.

"Mr M___ how good to see you. Have you come for a haircut?" Dumi asked, eager to serve the man who'd saved him.

"Not at all, young man. At my age looking stylish is not a preoccupation. I want to arrange something for the missus. Our wedding anniversary is just around the corner and ... well, you know how women like to be pampered. I was hoping there might something special you could do for her."

"What did you have in mind?"

"I don't know, perhaps you could suggest something for me."

Dumisani rubbed his chin. He was a man who knew how to pamper a woman and so we pricked up our ears waiting to hear what he would suggest.

"What day is the anniversary?"

"Tenth of December. That's when I signed away my independence." Mr M___ gave a wimpish laugh and then tried to regain his composure as no one laughed.

"We need to do something more than her hair. Tell you what, book her in for three hours: we'll do her hair, give her a facial, pedicure, manicure and an Indian head massage. It will give this salon a chance to branch out into beauty therapy."

"I don't know what you mean by all these things, just tell me how much it will cost."

"We'll have to charge you on the day because anything you give us now will be worthless by then."

"You're right of course."

"Let me take down your cell number just in case we need to talk beforehand." The look they exchanged as they took each other's cellphone numbers seemed odd to me, and if I hadn't known Dumi, it seemed a guilty one. Mr M___ had to repeat his twice as he seemed so nervous. Men nearly always felt uncomfortable in the very female atmosphere of a salon, but still his demeanour struck me as a little bizarre – he had been, after all, an intrepid guerrilla fighter.

***

We spent that night at the Ncubes' mansion. Lately we were spending more time there. Chiwoniso loved it because of the swimming pool and because they all doted on her. She even began to call the

Ncubes *sekuru* and *gogo*, grandpa and grandma. This pleased them no end and Mr Ncube took walks with her round the garden whenever he was not at work. Mrs Ncube tried to teach her to knit, a disastrous experiment that left the house with strands of wool everywhere.

Michelle was hopping about the place and told me I had a big surprise waiting for my birthday. At dinner I could see that she and her mother were dying to give me hints but could not because every time they looked as if they might, Mr Ncube coughed loudly and cleared his throat. When I went to bed that night Dumi came in and read me a bedtime story. It was called 'A Kiss for Little Bear' by Else Holmelund Minarik, Chiwoniso's favourite or so he told me. I could not sleep trying to figure out what it was they might have planned for me. I knew that whatever it was, I would never have enjoyed a day like it. They didn't know that this was the first time in my adult life that anyone had bothered to do something for me on my birthday.

"Rise and shine, sleeping beauty!" Michelle shouted and I woke with a start. She jumped on the bed and landed next to me with a bump. "You're always the first up, what's wrong with you today?"

"I couldn't get to sleep last night."

"Age is catching up with you. Look, there are even lines under your eyes. How gross!"

"I'm still only twenty-six."

"Leave her alone." Dumi walked in with a tray. He'd made me breakfast in bed. "Happy birthday." He kissed me.

"Thanks, you really shouldn't have. Where's Chiwoniso?"

"I've taken her to school already, we didn't want to wake you. Dumi, can you bring me some breakfast as well?"

"Get your own." He fled from the room.

I ate my breakfast and Michelle joined me. In fact she ate most of it. I couldn't keep up with her. Somehow she managed to eat, chew, swallow and talk at the same time. There was a knock on the door and she answered. Mr and Mrs Ncube came in in their pyjamas.

"Happy birthday, *muroora*," they said in unison, as if they'd rehearsed it.

"*Maita henyu.*" I clapped my hands.

"Finish your breakfast, we have to go to your surprise."

They left me with Michelle, but try as I may I could not extract the secret from her. She shut her eyes tightly, ran her hand across her mouth to zip it and threw away an imaginary key.

"They will kill me if I tell you," she said soon after that.

"Hey, your mouth is zipped up," I said.

"It's a magic zip that only allows me to say certain things."

***

After my shower I was blindfolded and led to the car. Dumi guided my every step making sure I did not bump into anything. I sat in the Merc feeling every bump and turn but unsure of where we were going. We could have been driving in circles for all I knew.

"My witchdoctor told me that if I want my businesses to prosper, I need to bring him some human body parts, so he can make me some *muti*," Mr Ncube said with a sinister laugh.

"We're going to turn you into mince-meat!" echoed Michelle.

"Stop scaring my poor *muroora*," said Mrs Ncube firmly.

"We're only kidding," Michelle said, pretending to be hurt.

"But this girl would make good *muti* " Mr Ncube pleaded in the same pretend voice he used for Chiwoniso.

"Thank God we've arrived," Mrs Ncube said.

Dumi opened the passenger door and guided me out of the car. I could hear the sound of cars so I knew we were still in the city, and I could hear the footfall of pedestrians. I walked slowly with fearful steps. I wasn't afraid of hurting myself if I fell down, it was the embarrassment of falling in a public place that worried me.

"Mind, we're going up a pavement," Dumi said. I negotiated the step and felt people brush past my shoulder. They must have wondered what this silly girl was doing with a blindfold on in the middle of the morning. We went up a couple of stairs and then back down again. I was feeling more and more disoriented. The buzz around us told me we were in a very busy place, but beyond that I could not make anything out except the delicious smell of freshly baked bread. It took me back to the days when Aroma used to sell fresh bread in Budiriro. Real bread made of flour and not the current stuff that was supplemented by maize meal, tasted vile and crumbled in your hands.

"Almost there now," Dumi said, his voice excited. Michelle had been talking non-stop to a point where none of us really heard her anymore. She didn't seem to mind when we didn't respond, and kept on regardless.

"Here we are. Remove the blindfold." Mr Ncube spoke in a boisterous voice as if he wanted the people going past to notice us.

The blindfold was gently removed. I opened my eyes and squinted to adjust to the light. I stood in a large empty shop with a large glass front. I looked left and right, nothing seemed familiar, and there was sharp smell of paint.

"What do you think?" Mrs Ncube asked.

"Of what?" I said slowly, worried that they might be disappointed by my lack of enthusiasm.

"Your new hairdresser's salon."

I opened my mouth but no sound came out. If Dumi had not gripped my arms, I'm sure I would have fainted. The Ncubes were beaming. People on the pavement had stopped to look at us. I fanned myself, tears in my eyes and my lips moving. I wanted to express my gratitude but couldn't find the right words. The pride on all their faces told me that they knew exactly how I felt.

"What are you going to call it?" asked Michelle.

Twenty-nine

Sam Levy's Village in Borrowdale is Harare's premier shopping centre. It was built with a certain sense of nostalgia for a small English town. Its two main rivals, Eastgate and Westgate, were newer but they lacked its character. Eastgate was located in the city centre, a place avoided by the new elite; Westgate with its Mediterranean aura failed to charm a nation for whom there was a passion for all things British and for whom English meant everything that was excellent in life.

Sam Levy's was built around a pedestrian thoroughfare with two rows of brown-bricked buildings with high-pitched roofs that gave them a sort of quaint fairy-tale feel. The only thing that did not have a British feel were the palm trees that lined the walkways, but no one seemed to mind. In any case, why shouldn't palm trees be British? The clock tower in the centre of the thoroughfare always told the right time, two hours ahead of GMT. Politicians mouthed anti-English rhetoric on TV by day and by night they came to shop at Sam Levy's Village because it was what they liked. During Operation Murambatsvina, when thousands of structures were declared illegal and arbitrarily demolished, Sam Levy's was discovered to have been built without proper planning permission. There was some talk about demolishing the whole structure, but how could they, since it provided a comfort zone for the new élite, an imaginary place of civilisation?

So the plans to pull it down were quietly shelved. No doubt money changed hands as well, but it was probably the only 'illegal' structure to survive in the entire city.

There was not a single shred of litter to be seen on the pavements. Cleaners walked idly round the centre, their only task being to sweep up leaves and other debris because no one in their right mind would dare drop litter on such pristine pavements.

Mrs Khumalo did not seem surprised when I told her that I was quitting to start my own business. She half advised and half discouraged me, saying the economy was not doing well and these times were very difficult to run a business.

Her parting shot was, "When you fail… sorry. If you fail, know that there will always be a job for a hairdresser of your calibre here." Yolanda secretly promised to come and work for me, once I was up and running. Charlie Boy was disappointed when I told him we had no plans for a barber. The one person that I really wanted with me was Dumi, who was rather vague, but said that he would hand in his notice before too long. I felt he was procrastinating but decided it was because he wanted me to stand on my own feet first.

I did not have the money to fit the shop out and buy the equipment I needed but Mr and Mrs Ncube had already worked that out for me.

"We've already covered your rent for the first quarter of the year, that's your gift. Buy all the equipment and products you need and you can return the loan interest-free in two years' time." It was more than a generous offer because in two years whatever amount he gave me now in Zim dollars would be less than worthless, and he didn't suggest we work out a price in hard currency. I figured that his gesture was calculated to ensure that my pride was not harmed. "It was tough for me when I started out in business and I wish someone had been there to guide me. If ever there is anything you need, do not hesitate to call on me. We are family."

I wanted the place open before Christmas and spent the first month with shop-fitters laying out the interior. It was harder work than I'd imagined. Michelle became my chauffeur and drove me to incessant appointments. We bought quality chairs, dryers and equipment. When the work was finished my salon was a brightly lit room with five chairs on one side and on the other, the stainless steel wash-basins. There was also a shelf with hair-care products and cosmetics for sale to clients. I only had a few posters on the walls because I did not want the salon to look tacky.

Already there were four established hairdresser's salons at Sam Levy's: Catt's Beauté, Devine Touch, Goddess Hair and Beauty Salon and the aptly named Village Beauty. Stiff competition. I needed a name. By mid-December all my signage had to be up. African Queen, Nubian, Essex … nothing seemed quite right. I wanted something that everyone would remember the very first time they heard it.

The hairdressing project consumed so much of my time that I worried I was neglecting Dumi and Chiwoniso. However, that they didn't seem to mind occasionally piqued me.

***

After we'd finished our chores, Michelle dropped me off at home early one day. I was surprised to see a Land Rover I didn't recognise in the driveway. Maidei had never brought visitors to the house before and I had assumed Dumi was at work. I unlocked the door cautiously, fearful that they would be robbers.

"Is anyone at home?" I called out from the doorway.

There was the sound of footsteps in the bedroom wing, so I shouted that I was going to call the police. What a bluff! Police vehicles never had any petrol, so I couldn't know when they would come, if at all.

"It's only me." I heard Dumi's voice calling from his room.

I relaxed. "I thought you were at work."

Dumi popped his head out of his room and replied, "I got my schedule mixed up. I wasn't supposed to be in work today."

"Whose car is that out there?"

He could not have heard me because he returned to his room. Could it be another woman? I chided myself for being so petty about the man I thought I loved.

A few minutes later Dumi emerged with someone behind him whom I could not see properly because the corridor light was dim.

"Mrs Proprietor herself. It's good to see you. I had feared I was going to leave without seeing you." The familiar voice was Mr M___'s.

"*Aizve!* I was not expecting you. Would you like me to cook you some sadza?" I stood up to greet him.

"Don't trouble yourself. I'd just dropped in to see this young man about our wedding anniversary, when he told me that you are opening your own salon soon."

"Yes, we're putting the finishing touches to it now. We hope to open on the fifteenth, in time for the Christmas rush."

"It's a pity you won't be ready in time for the anniversary though I doubt I could ever convince my wife to go anywhere else but Mrs Khumalo's."

"Maybe that will change when all her favourite hairdressers move there."

"I'm not a woman, so you would know better than me."

"Can I offer you a drink? Maidei, Maidei, where is this girl?" I stood up to go to the kitchen to find her.

"I gave her the afternoon off so she could go into town," Dumi said. This was the first time he had ever interfered with domestic affairs and I thought he was beginning to assert himself as the man of the house.

"I was just about to leave," Mr M___ said. "There is never any time to sit down and chat with people like we used to do in the old days. Right now I have to go to a Party meeting and from there I'm off to the farm. I tell you, I'm far too old for this. Dumisani, we should talk about our surprise a bit more if you get a chance. I need this thing to be perfect."

***

That evening I lay in bed with Dumi and we chatted about the new salon's business model. I needed to set it apart and give it higher standards than anything else at the centre.

"Look at the people who go there. They're wealthy and flashy and often wear bling, so you need to take them to the next level. Whatever they charge, you charge double. It will cream off the wealthiest and give them the exclusivity they're always craving."

So that's how the name for my salon was born – Exclusive.

Thirty

The day my salon opened was the best day of my life. There was a purple sign at the front which read – Exclusive, in bold cursive lettering. It wasn't Exclusive Hairdressers or Exclusive Hairdressing and Beauty, no, my salon was just Exclusive. Michelle and another girl wore shorts and t-shirts advertising the salon and handed out small business cards with our phone number, which on one side read, *Exclusive,* and on the other, *We Don't Want You.*

There were stickers on the window stating, 'By appointment only'. I sat in the shop sipping champagne with the Ncubes. The first people who came were stopped by two suited men in dark glasses at the front who told them the salon would not be open to the public until the first VIP came in to get her hair done. The more people they turned away, the more arrived to try to find out what was going on.

This first customer was due in at half past ten and I paced the floor anxiously, praying she would show up. The manager of the complex came to check that everything was all right for our grand opening. A photographer from the *Herald* stopped by to take a few photos and wandered around the shopping centre waiting for our guest to arrive.

"You look a bundle of nerves, child. Try to relax," Mrs Ncube said as she adjusted my waistcoat. I'd decided that our uniform would comprise black trousers, white blouses and purple waistcoats with the logo of a woman sitting cross-legged in a yoga position.

"Are you sure she's coming?"

"They wouldn't be here if she wasn't." Mrs Ncube pointed at the suited men.

My palms were sweaty and I had to wipe them every few minutes with one of our towels. Dumi was with us as well. He had taken a fortnight off work and decided to postpone his holiday until the new year. His visa was valid for six months in any case. My new receptionist/cashier was at the desk. She was Trina's cousin, Sarah, a woman with fiery red hair who spoke with a Rhodie accent and was great at organising the admin aspects of the business.

"I always knew you'd start up your own place one day," said Trina who'd come to see the opening. She had agreed to be my supplier, but only if I guaranteed there wouldn't be any war vets visiting the shop.

"I had a lot of help." I gestured towards the Ncubes.

"Nonsense girl, Exclusive is not the place for false modesty." Mr Ncube laughed so loudly, the sound reverberated round the walls.

The shop had five staff including Sarah: Dumi, who still needed to give his notice to Mrs Khumalo, Yolanda, a girl called Tariro who I'd poached from Central Hair, and me. We would get more staff as and when the business expanded. In the meantime Sarah could help out on the floor when needed.

The phone rang and everyone fell silent. It was our first call already.

Sarah picked it up. "Yallo … You want an appointment… let me see… hmm… when did you want to come in… mmm not today or tomorrow… this week is tight but we could fit you in on Friday…"

The truth is we had no appointments in the book but Dumi had told her to make it seem as though we were inundated. "The illusion of success is enough to breed success," he'd said authoritatively. Sarah put the receiver down. She'd put on a convincing performance. I just hoped that the stunt wouldn't backfire and cost us customers. She winked as she gave me the thumbs up.

"The first one's in the bag."

I looked at the clock and it was twenty-five to eleven. Our guest still hadn't shown up. I could hear my tummy rumble and feel the butterflies floating inside. What if she doesn't show? Dumi patted my shoulder to comfort me.

Outside a man and a woman appeared in front of the shop. They pointed at the sign as if unsure of where they were. The woman wore a yellow and white doek and had a similar cloth wrapped around her waist like a village woman. The man wore a faded grey suit, which had seen too many days, and walked with a slight stoop. Behind them a security guard followed at a distance, observing them. They looked out of place in an upmarket area like this.

"*Pamwe ndipo,*" the woman said, and they approached the shop. The security men stopped them and told them the place was only open for people with appointments. That's when I recognised them.

"*Baba, amai,*" I shouted and ran to the door. "Let them pass," I said to the guards.

"Is it really you my daughter?" my mother said, her eyes moistening. I embraced them both and tried hard to stop myself crying.

"Fungai told us you were opening a shop and we came to see for ourselves. God be praised." My father's eyes wandered about the shop with pride.

I introduced them to Mr and Mrs Ncube who seemed relieved that there was a couple of their own age to converse with. They clapped their hands and said "*makadini*" to one another as tradition dictated. Their conversation quickly veered to the subject of their rural homes. As with all old people they quickly came up with some obscure connection that immediately made them distant relatives. If my parents had made the effort to break with our dispute and come and celebrate with me then I had every right to feel invincible. Nothing could possibly go wrong except that the guest was half an hour late and we were all getting restless.

Michelle ran into the salon around half past eleven and shouted, "Battle stations people, Auntie Grace is coming."

A few seconds later, the president's wife walked in, surrounded by four bodyguards. She wore a black suit with golden embroidery running down the hem of the skirt and all around the borders of the jacket. She had an elegant walk and took no notice of the people gawking at her from the pavements. The *Herald* reporter returned just in time to snap her as she walked through the door.

"*Tisvikewo* – May I come in?" she said on the threshold. Dumi pushed me forward to meet her, saying it was my big day.

"Please come in, Amai Mugabe," I said with a curtsy.

"Call me Auntie Grace. Amai Mugabe makes me sound so old." She beamed at me with a gracious smile. "It's Vimbai, isn't it?"

She already knew the Ncubes and greeted them. I went round and introduced my parents who were overwhelmed to be in her presence. Her apparently easy-going nature made them feel at ease, especially when she called them *Amai* and *Baba*. The last person I introduced was Trina. She was at the back and the strain showed on her face.

"Are you related to Nick Price the golfer by any chance?" Auntie Grace asked her.

"As a matter of fact I am." Trina masked the hostility in her voice well.

"There's also Ray Price the cricketer, you're all related aren't you? No one has done more than the Prices to put the Zimbabwean flag on the sporting map. You should take my phone number down. If I can be of any use to you in the future do not hesitate to call me." A slight smile appeared on Trina's face but vanished quickly as if she was afraid to hope.

We sat Auntie Grace in the chair near the window and gave her a cup of coffee.

"Your prices are scary," she said with a laugh. "Tell me exactly what you are going to do to me Vimbai before you rob me."

Everyone went silent waiting for me to talk. Dumi crossed his fingers and mouthed something like – go girl.

"I'm going to make you look good for the President." Grace laughed and everyone else laughed along with her.

"That's a tall order, your president is a hard man to please."

"This is the easiest job I will ever do because his wife is already stunningly beautiful." When I said this Auntie Grace looked at herself in the mirror with a hint of vanity. "Your face has strong well-defined features. I'm going to give you braids that match the complexion of your skin." I took out four packets and matched each one against her face until I settled on a rusty coloured one. "Dumi, come over to the other side and work with me."

We worked furiously weaving the braids into her hair. We left the ends free just as Dumi had done for Minister M___. Auntie Grace sat patiently and chatted with the Ncubes. With the both of us working together, we finished her in half the time it would normally have taken. She looked at herself in the mirror and turned from side to side nodding her head to show her satisfaction. When she tried to get up from the chair I ordered her back down. We then went on to give her a pedicure and a manicure. This was built into our bill, but because we didn't announce it, the client would leave the chair thinking that it had been done specially for them.

"I feel like a new woman. Thank you very much. This is all so lovely. Now Vimbai, I can't come here every month but I would like you to be my personal hairdresser from now on. I will call for you whenever I need you." Everyone applauded when she said this.

As soon as she left the salon with her suited companions I collapsed on the chair.

Thirty-one

The salon really took off in the new year. I figured since the country's average life expectancy was thirty-seven, I would concentrate on the young and the beautiful. There was no point in indulging a clientele that was statistically supposed to be dead. For people over forty we were very selective; they had to be the cream of the elite to use our service.

The publicity garnered from the first lady's visit had been of immense value to us. Our salon had been featured in the state newspapers and the independent weeklies. The latter did not know that they were doing us a favour in their portrayal of the salon as over-priced and elitist.

It became necessary for me to spend more and more time at the business. I had also begun taking driving lessons because I needed my own wheels. Dumi had served his notice at Mrs Khumalo's salon. He told me she had practically begged him to stay. We were spending less time together but I was so happy in my work that I did not notice his absence or question it as I might once have done. I hoped that once he had begun working for me our companionship would resume.

***

The first time I felt something was wrong was toward the end of January. We were both at home when a car pulled up at the gate late at night.

"I'm going out tonight, I'll be back later," Dumi said putting on a jacket.

"Who is it?" I asked, wondering why he had not mentioned that he was going out before.

"No one, just a friend that's all. We're just nipping out for a drink."

"It's almost midnight and you have work tomorrow."

"I'll be back."

I watched him walk across the driveway in the glare of the headlights. It gave him an eerie look. I could not figure out whose car it was. Was it another woman? Come to think of it, on a few occasions, Dumi had often taken to going to his bedroom when his phone rang and speaking in a low voice. Surely Dumi wouldn't betray me! I felt guilty even thinking this way, and he'd given me so much support.

Had I been taking him for granted? I didn't think so, but it was true we hardly ever spoke about our future together now; it was like something given.

I could not sleep, tossing and turning in my sheets, trying to figure out what was going on. It was true that all the time we'd been together Dumi had not once introduced me to any of his 'friends', yet he'd been comfortable enough to introduce me to his family. Now, thinking about it, it seemed odd. I knew that in the middle of the night problems have a way of growing exponentially, but I could not shake off my anxiety. I'd kept my curtains open and my ears pricked every time I heard a car passing by. Part of me wanted to go into his room to search for clues but I controlled myself.

At three o'clock in the morning, Dumi had still not returned. Four o'clock and I paced round the living room occasionally peering out into the dark hoping to see him emerging through the garden. He was not the kind of person to cheat, it didn't seem in character. Perhaps he was preparing a surprise for me. What if he had been in an accident while I was imagining all sorts of acts of betrayal and deceit. I felt ashamed of myself.

Day broke and I went for a bath. By the time I left for work, he still had not returned. It was raining heavily and my umbrella broke in the wind, so when I arrived to open the shop I was drenched to the bone. Sarah came in soon afterwards, her hair soaked, looking like a wet dog.

"Morning, Baas," she said, reaching for a towel and drying herself.

"The farmers will be pleased today."

"If they're farming anything other than weeds maybe."

Holding a cup of coffee, I looked out over the drenched grey atmosphere. This was surely what Britain looked like. Robert had once told me about the grey overcast skies and the coldness of the people there.

"What's on your mind, lovey?"

"Nothing," I replied.

"Don't give me that. I'm slightly older and wiser than you. Let me guess, man troubles is it?"

I gave a weary smile and sipped my coffee.

"That Dumisani of yours seems a decent chap, not like the other black guys I've seen who always seem to have another woman somewhere. No offence meant."

"He went out and didn't come home last night."

"Oh." She covered her mouth with her hand. "There could be a rational explanation for it."

"That's what I'm hoping."

She patted my hand in a motherly gesture and poured herself a cup of tea. People were running by trying to stay out of the rain. We would have talked some more if Yolanda and Tariro had not come in. They were also drenched and I told them to spruce themselves up. The first customer would be coming in at any moment. It was a struggle but I wore my business face.

I got home with a heavy heart. Chiwoniso jumped on me and showed me a picture she had drawn at school. It had me, a big woman with wild hair drawn in purple with a pink triangle for a skirt, her as a miniature version of me and a man, Dumi, standing tall between the two of us, his afro represented by a mass of curly lines.

"It's a really good drawing, but where is Sisi Maidei?" I said to her.

"She is that one." She pointed to the woman in the triangle skirt.

"Where's mummy?"

"Mummy's at work."

I set her on the ground but she ran off to her room to play with her toys. I did not know what to make of that. The business had consumed me so much. I was spending less time with my daughter. Maidei came in to give me some letters. They were the electricity bill and council rates for the coming months. It felt good not to be in arrears any more. I looked at Maidei standing before me and for the first time realised that she held a special place in my daughter's heart. She was there for her when I was not. Only now did I realise how important she was in my life. If Maidei was not there, I could not have accomplished half the things I had done over the last few years. I'd spent all my time thinking of her as a simpleton. When was the last time I said thank you to her?

"Is Dumi in?" I asked.

"He should be in his room."

"What time did he come back?"

"Around ten o'clock this morning."

"What did he do after that?"

"He went straight to bed."

I dismissed Maidei and sat alone in the lounge. One part of me wanted to go immediately to his room to confront him but I was too angry and afraid I would say the wrong things, stuff I would regret later on. I tried to remember our long forgotten auntie's advice for dealing with errant men but it did not come to me. Anger was never the answer. I told Maidei not to bother cooking, I would do it myself. I prepared a course of spicy chicken with plenty of soup and rice. The stomach was the way into a man's heart.

Dumi woke up after eight and I invited him to have dinner with me at the table. I had already sent Chiwoniso to bed so we were alone.

"It smells really nice," he said as he sat down. "Candlelit dinner, what's the special occasion?"

"I cooked it myself."

"You know how much I love your cooking; maybe after the salon, you'll open a restaurant."

Dumi devoured his food almost without tasting it, and asked for more. He washed the chicken down with a glass of cold water. I ate slowly and with each mouthful I felt as though I would gag. Dumi could not look me in the face. Whenever I tried to make eye contact, he looked at his empty plate.

"I think we need to talk," I said finally. He scratched his nose with his pinkie.

"Sure thing, you know we can talk about anything."

"Let's start with who you were with last night."

"I already told you I was out with a friend."

"What's her name?"

"His name is Paul, we went to school together."

"Where did you go?"

"Um… just to the club for a drink. Chez Ntemba."

"I never took you for a Rhumba fan. What time did you get back?"

"I came in just after you'd left and rushed straight out to go to work. Look, this is beginning to sound like an interrogation…"

Thirty-two

Jealousy is the worst feeling in the world. It creeps up on you, hugs you so that you can't breathe. Your chest feels compressed and food loses its taste. In my case my condition was worsened by uncertainty. In the morning Dumi greeted me and told me he'd made breakfast himself since I'd cooked him dinner. He adjusted the bun in Chiwoniso's hair before Maidei walked her to school. His expression impregnable, I was at a loss. He seemed the same old Dumi that I knew and loved. We talked about new styles emerging from the backyard salons in Highfields and Canaan and wondered if we could convert them to look upmarket.

"You're still on course for joining me at the end of this month aren't you?"

"Of course, nothing has changed." He spoke through a mouthful of toast. I wondered if he was right. Perhaps nothing was something and then what?

We left for work together. There were more cars on the road because the petrol situation had improved. The government was allowing more stations to sell their petrol in foreign currency and that had eased the acute shortages. The kombi we took was full and we hung on for dear life near the door, which seemed about to fall off.

"When are you going to buy your licence? There's no way you'll catch me taking two kombis every day to Sam Levy's!"

"Give me to the end of February. The instructor wants me to take the test in Chinhoyi because that's where his connections are. You still have to pass through the drums and parallel parking but once you are out of the VID depot and on the road, the licence is guaranteed."

"No wonder we have the highest accident rates in the world. They should just stop the charade and start selling the damn licences in supermarkets, or at auctions to the highest bidder."

"Everyone's doing it."

"That's precisely the problem. If they set the standards they're supposed to set, the whole practice would stop. There's no way they could fail each and every person coming through their door. I've sat two tests and been failed twice because I won't pay a bribe. I was raised in a car and I know the rules of the road better than any of those jokers but they still fail me. Even the instructors are in on it. They get a cut too. The whole thing stinks."

Could someone who was so upright cheat me? It didn't seem possible. I wanted to kiss him on the cheek when we parted but it was too public. I felt as if I'd been torn in half, become two people with two different minds and two different hearts.

Sarah was waiting for me outside the shop when I arrived. I resolved to give her a set of keys, in case one day I was delayed or fell ill. She was always the first of my staff to come on site and the last to leave. "Have you found out anything else about his mysterious whereabouts?" she asked as I let her in.

"Nothing yet but I'm sure there's something he's not telling me."

"Sounds a little like my ex-husband."

"You never told me you had a husband."

"I said 'ex'. I was married at twenty-one. You know, that age when love is supposed to last a lifetime and you feel all warm and fuzzy inside. It lasted just five years and I'm glad to be out of it."

"Where did it all go wrong?"

"Cheating of course. There are only two certainties in a relationship, either he cheats on you or you're going to cheat on him at some point. Hear this from someone with experience; men can't keep their dicks in their pants."

"But Dumi is..."

"It's the ones you least expect that hurt you the most. Relationships are a game of cat and mouse. Now you're the pussy but you have to behave more like the guard dog. He has to realise that if he's up to no good, you'll know, no matter how discreet he is. Put the fear of God up his arse."

"Do you really think that would work?"

"Not really... with my ex I put spyware on the computer and on his mobile so I would know every text he received, every e-mail, everything. It was some MacGyver stunt, real FBI. And spying made me feel pretty cheap, I can tell you. Still, he knew that I knew but he went ahead and did what he did. That's because when sex gets into their heads they just can't help themselves, I mean he left me for some Irish floozy who'd come down here on holiday – can you believe that?" She opened the diary and the receipt book to prepare for the day.

Our kombi journey had somehow lulled my anxieties. Now, talking about the situation brought them all back. Sarah made me a cup of tea and I felt a little bit better.

"Dumi is the one, I can't even begin to imagine a future without him. He's a great listener and I think he would make a great father for Chiwoniso." My head felt light like someone had blown hot air inside it. Sarah leant towards me and offered her hand.

"I don't know what I can tell you but the best advice I can give is stay on your toes. Keep one step ahead because once you start reacting, you've lost the battle." She spoke like a woman whose heart has been torn to pieces, and who wasn't going to that dark place ever again. She rubbed her naked ring finger as if it was itchy.

Michelle dropped into the salon around closing time. She had come to take me home, which she did every so often. It gave us a chance to catch up and gossip. She was wearing blue track bottoms and we went over to Mimi's for a coffee. The owner recognised me and asked how the salon was doing.

"It's very pricey, that Exclusive of yours."

"But look at how much you're charging us for coffee beans and boiling water," Michelle said with a smirk.

"You're getting more than that. There's the ambience which you won't get anywhere else."

"Maybe you should come down to the salon one day and we'll pamper you, then you'll see that we also offer an ambience you can't get anywhere else."

She left us and went back behind the counter. Each time someone spoke to me like this I felt part of the family at Sam Levy's. We were all peddling smoke and mirrors and worried that one day someone would pull the rug out from under our feet. The smell of the coffee filled my nostrils. There's something vaguely erotic about having coffee and I think it came from all the *Sex and the City* I was watching on my new satellite channels.

"So how's things between you and Dumi?"

"All right, I guess."

"Just all right? My brother is super, you should be looking after him."

"I am."

"Anyway you two are boring, so let's skip that. I met a guy today. He's really hot. I was kinda bored and hanging around the gate at home when this guy on a mountain bike stops and asks the time. I was like, damn! To cut a long story short he gave me his number and we've been texting all day." As if on cue her phone began to vibrate.

"Is it him?"

"He says he was just thinking about me. I-WAS-THINKING-ABOUT-YOU-TOO. This guy has to be the one."

"You're a bit too young for that. What does he do for a living anyway."

"He's at uni in Australia studying architecture or something like that. I think I might go over to do my uni there too if mum and dad allow me. There's no way they'll cough up if they think it's for a guy."

When I returned home Dumi told me that he was going away to Nyanga for the weekend. He needed a break and some fresh air and wanted to go mountain climbing while he was there. I waited for an invitation that never came.

Thirty-three

On Friday morning Dumi packed his bags and left for the Eastern Highlands. He kissed my cheek as though it was obligatory and off he went without once looking back. I'd taken the weekend off and left Sarah to run the salon. Though I knew what I had to do, I dreaded finding something that would confirm my suspicions. Feeling this way seemed like a sign of my own weakness, a sign of how quickly I was ready not to trust the man who had loved me and given me everything I had until now.

I could not even begin to contemplate what I would do if I found something out. My life and my daughter's future were tied to the magnanimity of the Ncube family. There could be no guarantee that their kindness would outlast my relationship with their son. These thoughts made me feel like a gold-digger. I'd loved Dumi even when I had thought he was as ordinary as myself, but looking back it became blurry as to whether it would have gone this far if I had not found out about his privileged background. Sure, it has kind of added to the fairy-tale ... but I wasn't certain that I wanted to go down this route. What was I thinking? My parents now knew about him of course and this further complicated matters. They had only just come back into my life and I didn't want any scandal that might complicate my relationship with them.

The postman rode past our house on his red bicycle. Apart from the sound of his tyres on the road, I felt an ominous stillness. I'd been raised in a house full of people with very little privacy so it was something I valued. I knew Dumi had a right to his as well, but wasn't that overridden by my right to know the truth? AIDS was another consideration, so if he was cheating then I had a right to protect myself.

I knew I was being illogical, even self-rightous. How could he be cheating when he'd refused to sleep with me because he wanted us to wait until we were married? I had been charmed at the time but now I found myself asking what type of man, even a Catholic man, was it who refused the prospect of sex offered him on a silver platter? There was, after all, a chance he was looking after himself since Phillip was a well-known philanderer – perhaps Dumi feared that I carried the dreaded virus in my blood.

The more I thought, the more I found myself confused and perplexed. Yet Dumi had lied to me about where he was the other night. If he'd had nothing to hide he would surely have told me the truth. I had a duty not only to myself, but to my daughter who now saw him as a father figure. It was still early out I went to the kitchen and poured myself a glass of red wine and drank it in one go. Then I picked up the whole bottle and took it with me to the lounge where I began to drink it straight. The wine tasted like straw and I forced it down. It went to work immediately. I had drunk it on an empty stomach and the alcohol raced into my bloodstream, and straight to my head.

"Maidei, I want you to go to town," I said as soon as she appeared.

"Sure, what would you like me to go and get?"

"That's none of your business. I want you to get out of this house and go to town." I was slurring but could not control it. The poor girl gave me a wide-eyed look and went slowly to the door. She must have thought it was some kind of obedience test.

"Are you okay, Mama?" she asked timidly, her hand on the handle as though ready to flee.

"I'm not your mother, stupid. Get out of my house." She went out slowly and shut the door behind her. The poor wretch was completely in my power. I fed her, clothed her and sheltered her. Her entire existence was dependent on my slightest whim. Such is the life of a house-girl living in perpetual awe of the mistress of the house. I called her back and threw some money at her, telling her to buy herself a new dress. She clapped her hands and left looking very confused.

When I got up from my seat I felt as if the world was turning at an incredible speed. The floor under me did a sort of dance that made me fall back into my chair. I got up and began to navigate my way across the treacherous ground, reaching out to hold the walls for added support. I took a few steps into the corridor and dropped to the ground with a thud. It was as though I was learning to walk again. It took supreme determination for me to rise once more and walk. Each single step I took felt as though I had covered a thousand miles.

Dumi's bedroom was right at the end of the corridor past a Jesus poster with eyes that followed you wherever you went. I reached his door and opened it. His bed was neatly made. The toiletries on his chest of drawers were arranged in two straight lines. Even the dirty laundry was folded and placed in the corner. Dumi did his own washing and would not let Maidei do it. I glanced around the room and saw nothing amiss. Part of the problem was that I did not know exactly what I was looking for.

I checked under the bed, under his pillows, nothing there. There were so many clothes in his wardrobe, I went through each shelf and every pocket of his trousers and found nothing there as well. Something told me I would be rewarded if I kept up my frantic search. I leant on the window sill and thought. Then I staggered back to his bed and raised his mattress. Underneath was a small black journal with 'Dumisani Ncube' written in silver lettering on the sleeve. I knew I had found what I was looking for.

***

I must have passed out because when I came to I was lying face down on the bed, a tiny pool of red vomit beside me. I got up slowly and wiped my mouth on the sheet. My head was thumping and the clock on the wall said it was one o'clock. I could hear Chiwoniso playing somewhere in the garden.

In my left hand I held the black diary. I surveyed the room: there were clothes all over the floor. Bottles of lotion spilt on the carpet. The whole place had been ransacked. I bundled up the soiled sheets and threw them into a heap on the side then sat back down on the bare mattress.

I opened the first page of the diary and closed it again. There was still a chance for me to do the right thing. 'Put it back in its place. It is not for you to know the secrets another has not chosen to reveal to you,' one voice said; another told me it was my house and I had every right to know whatever happened inside it. No matter how much I rationalised things, I still knew that what I was doing was wrong. I set off to work cleaning the room. I folded his clothes and placed them back in the wardrobe. The jackets and shirts that needed hanging I hung next to them. Dumi was observant and a perfectionist, he could not fail to notice that an intruder had been in his room and changed everything. I could not tell what I had got wrong but it all felt so different.

The last thing I picked up was his green passport. I flicked through it and saw stamps for Namibia, Mozambique, New Zealand, Botswana, Kenya and several for South Africa. All this travel had taken place in the last four years. The last was his visa to the UK, which I stroked; I wished he'd asked me to go with him. I thought of my own new passport so bare and unloved. There was a good reason for holding onto my man no matter what it took. I was doing this for us, I kept telling myself.

I met Maidei in the corridor as I stepped out of the room. She averted her gaze, disapproving but powerless to question what she knew I had done.

"Maswera sei." Her voice was wary, disapproving.

"There are some sheets on Dumi's bedroom floor. I want you to pick them up together with his laundry and wash everything." I heard the hostility in my voice, it was as if I was blaming her for everything I had done, for my drunkenness, my shame, her disapproval ... everything.

I walked past her into the safety of my own bedroom. When I shut the door I must have shut out what remained of my conscience. I opened the diary to claim my prize of the truth. Even now I wish I never had, the contents were worse than anything I could ever have imagined.

Thirty-four

After a moment of hesitation I began to read. It seems the diary had been started some time in the year prior to when we first met:

October 6
Great weekend with Colin at Troutbeck. Never knew trout fishing could be so much fun. ... Colin caught a big one whilst I seemed to pull out frog after frog. There must have been something dodgy about my bait. Did some horse riding through trails in the pine treed forests...

More entries of a similar nature followed. Dumi never seemed to be short of money and the two of them gallivanted all over the place, but another entry caught my eye.

December 3
Spent the weekend at home with Colin. We decided not to go anywhere. No man has ever made me feel so good about myself. He's trying to persuade me to return to Canada with him ... am very tempted.

Then there seemed to be a gap of months.

March 10

Where to begin? How to begin? So much has happened. All of it bad bad bad. My life feels hollow and no one to turn to or to talk to except you, little black book, but I've learned that even talking to myself provides some comfort. The sound of the door breaking and booted footsteps still wakes me at night. I can still hear the sound of his screams as he was dragged from bed and bundled into a van. There is no doubt in my mind that it was father who sent them. What business did they have when his visa still had two months left on it? And then his deportation for visa irregularities, which were never fully explained. He knew and I knew what it was all about.

The terrible thing that I can never explain to him is that my father was behind it all.

Don't know who it was that tipped him off, one of his ZANU cronies perhaps, there were plenty of them at the Great Zimbabwe hotel when we were there last ... maybe Kasuvandu saw us together in the bar late one night our arms round each other. The irony of it, he was there with a fleshy young woman, who was clearly not his wife, after all ...

But that my break from my family should come this way ... and on top of Colin's peremptory departure – I think he knew my family was behind it ... will he ever trust me again ...

March 22
Have made huge effort to pull myself together again. At least I know I can earn my living as a hairdresser, if anyone will take me –

April 01
Moved in with a colleague. Couldn't afford to pay rent at the house in Avondale anymore since allowance got cut off. I don't even think that she likes me. Didn't know being broke could be such a drag. My kingdom for a swimming pool!

May 23
Missing my family so much. Patrick getting married next month. I have lost everything. Need to make peace with Vimbai. Don't think she liked the fact that I got promoted over her. Her work is superb but she needs to do her styling from the soul. She is too mechanical, she thinks making her clients feel like 'white women' is the key, but what she actually needs to do

is to make them feel like women. Thinking of telling her but don't wanna mess with the landlady... Hope she forgives me but I need the extra cash from the job just to pay her rent. Due again next week...

June 05
Patrick getting married tomorrow. Haven't been sleeping as much as I should. Lay awake in bed all night reading Oscar Wilde's Dorian Gray. Flowery prose might just put me to sleep... Doesn't work. Vimbai and I getting along now. How will things go with the family? Praying to John Bradburne...

June 29
Can't believe how well things are going. Family utterly adores Vimbai, she's bigger than Michael Jackson. Allowance has been restored. Still keeping the job because I love it, but it feels so good not to have to look at the price tags when I go shopping. Need to tell Vimbai everything. Is it too soon? Seems like a really nice person. Don't know who to trust any more... It's way too risky. Need a bit more time. Get to know each other better. Can't afford to mess this up. Shouldn't have to live my life in the shadows like this.

August 02
Complete disaster! Now Chiwoniso is involved in all this. Have strong feelings for both mother and daughter. Want them to be in my life. Have to say something before things get too complicated. What am I saying? Things are already too complicated. Think, think. They have a right to know the truth. Must act soon...

September 13
Met strong, dashing man who literally saved my life...

The things I read made me drop the diary as if it were scalding my hand and I covered my mouth as if in prayer.

Thirty-five

"Is everything all right, Mummy? I heard you crying." Chiwoniso was standing at my door holding her favourite teddy bear.

"Everything's fine, sweetie. Go and play, mummy is just busy right now."

"But I want to play with you."

"Give me five minutes."

I looked at the diary on my floor. The tiny figure of my daughter lingered for a moment and then shut the door. DUMI IS A HOMO-SEXUAL – *Ngochani.* If it wasn't written in his hand and before my eyes, I would have denied it. I could not have foreseen this. He spoke like a normal man, wore clothes like a normal man and even walked like a normal man. Everything about him was masculine. Didn't homosexuals walk about with handbags and speak with squeaky voices?

I had to find out more. I scrunched my nose when I picked up the diary as if it smelt of something putrid. The page was open where I'd left it. What happened next right under my nose astonished me. The day I came home and found him and Mr M___ at my house was the day they had consummated their unnatural passions in the bed that I had shared with Dumi. I rubbed my body feeling dirty and needing a long bath. Which one of them was the man and which was the woman anyway? The journal did not shed any light on this.

166

As far as I knew, Dumi had been raised in a good Christian family (if Catholics are Christians) and here he was turning my house into his own Sodom and Gomorrah. It seems the Canadian fellow, Colin, was a pervert as well. The authorities should have arrested him and locked him up forever. For as long as I can remember there'd been rumours of white tourists coming into the country and corrupting the youth, but I thought they preyed on street children and beggars. I could gather from the journal that in fact there seemed to be an underground scene right beneath our noses where these depraves congregated. It was that GALZ movement that set up secret safe houses all across the city to encourage this sort of satanic behaviour. Surely not Dumi I felt numb.

The passages that were by far the sickest were the ones in which he declared his love for Mr M___, as if such a thing were ever possible. He used passionate terms like 'the love of my life', which only men and women should use. I reached for my Bible to give me strength as I went through the document leaf by leaf. They'd met many times, going off to secret locations where they pretended to be related. No one batted an eyelid if two men rented a hotel room, they would just think them relatives and leave it at that. I wondered who else knew about this. The journal was at pains to hide the names of other people, using only initials. I wondered why Dumi had done this when Colin and Mr M___ were named, and anyone who wanted to could target them or blackmail them.

"Mummy I want to play," Chiwoniso called from the other side of the door.

"I'm still busy, go and play with Sisi Maidei."

My daughter had been the product of the union between man and woman. What could a man and a man ever hope to produce in a million years? Even the president had called them worse than pigs – I might have disagreed with a lot of what he has done to the country but I had to agree with him there. Even now I imagined Mr M___ with his silly moustache fondling the man who was my fiancé.

"Okay, I'm coming," I said at last, as Chiwoniso kept calling at the door.

I could not sleep that night because of what I knew. I spent the whole of Saturday trying to recover from the blow. In my mind Phillip the rapist was better than Dumi the homo. I drank cup after cup of tea as if it could wash me clean of what I knew. I had a day before the pervert came back to my house. Many scenarios played in my head. I would call his parents over and when he arrived we would all be there to confront him. The thought that I had fallen for him made me feel like a person who had been duped of their lifesavings by a conman. Even that would be better than this. What would I tell my parents when they asked about him? The whole world would have a laugh at my expense. 'She was so bad that she drove him into the arms of a man.' Crude jokes like that would be made behind my back.

If it was another woman, I would fight to save my relationship, but another man! There is no response to that. It is the sort of thing that is so far outside of nature it can never happen. Even animals have sense enough to tell which one is female and which one is not. I opened my window to let the stale air out. There was a blast of cool air rushing in as if to cleanse my house. It was sweet and refreshing. If I hadn't a daughter to look after that day I should have ended my life. The shame of it all was enough to kill me. I couldn't sleep a wink again that night.

Sunday came and I rushed to church. I was the first one in the cinema and waited. Pastor Mvumba came in and was surprised to see me there.

"My daughter in Christ, what is troubling you that you should be so early?" The Pastor spoke as if the Holy Spirit was telling him about my troubles.

"Everything is just fine," I lied. I could not get myself to seek his counsel on such a delicate matter.

"What's your name again? I often see you in the congregation but you always leave before the end."

"Vimbai."

"Well then Vimbai, come down here and help me to arrange these newsletters."

That day I did not hear a single thing in the service. The singing and the prayers all whizzed past me. My mind was with someone else. The seat next to me was empty – that was where Dumi should have been if he had come with me.

That night I helped Chiwoniso with her homework. She had been assigned to read a few pages in her reading book, which she did placing a finger underneath one word and pronouncing it slowly. I found it a painful exercise and wondered how teachers were patient enough to endure it on their salaries.

"That's it, we're finished now."

"Two more pages, Mummy."

"No, your teacher said you should read up to page ten."

"But Uncle Dumi always lets me read extra."

"It's time for you to go to bed. Maidei, come and take her to bed." She had to be dragged kicking and screaming because she did not want to go. Raising her would only get more difficult the older she grew.

I sent Maidei off to bed early as well and told her to leave the dishes until the morning. I did not want anyone to be there when Dumi came in. The lights were switched off and I sat in the dark on the sofa nearest the door. The ticking clock made the only audible sound in the room. I counted every second until I heard the sound of the key in the door. It creaked open and his dark figure came in and locked it. He walked across the room to the corridor and that's when I called him.

"Christ! You startled me." He switched on the light. "What are you doing in the dark?"

I did not give him an answer. I just glared at him, hating his handsome face the longer I stared.

"What's up Vimbai? Coz this is kind of freaky," he said with the chortle that I once found cute, but now thought the vilest possible sound a human being could ever make. He was studying my face trying to read my mind. He put the satchel he was carrying on the ground and walked slowly toward me, one cautious step after the other. When he was just two steps away, I pulled out the journal from underneath the cushion.

His eyes widened and he took a step back, slipped by me, opened the door so fast that I didn't even see him unlock it, and ran off into the dark night.

***

I shall regret the next thing I did for as long as I live.

Thirty-six

The minister was sitting at her desk wearing reading glasses and signing document after document when I went in. She glanced at me dismissively and returned to her work. It had taken me perseverance and over two hours to get past security so I could see her. She occupied a corner office in Construction House on Leopold Takawira Street. Her hand moved with a flourish over the paper and I felt as invisible as a gnat.

"If you're expecting me to come to your new salon, Vimbai, then you should know I can't do it. Loyalty is very important. It pays to stick with your choices sometimes." She looked up at me, took off her glasses and put them on the table.

"That's not what I have come here for." My voice broke.

"Then what can I help you with? My receptionist says you were very adamant and you would not tell anyone else what this was about."

"I have a good reason."

"Out with it then. I am very busy."

"It is about Mr M___ and Dumi." I fished in my handbag and placed the journal on her table.

"What is this?"

"I think you better read it for yourself."

She squinted her eyes and then perched her reading glasses on the end of her nose. She sighed as she read through it, muttering 'not again' to herself. It seemed ages before she took off her glasses, but this time she kept them in her hand. There was an anguished look on her face but after a moment she regained her composure.

"Who else knows about this?"

"You are the first person I came to."

"I always thought you were a clever girl." She stood up and went to stand by the large window that ran from corner to corner intersecting with another at a right angle. "Are you absolutely certain there is no one else who knows this?"

"I am sure."

"This whole country is in a mess. I look down from my window every day and see it. To the right is your downtown. An area I wouldn't advise you to visit, it is filthy, full of crime and vice that runs all the way to Mbare, the beating heart, an example of everything that is wrong with this nation. On the other side you have First Street, Karigamombe and roads that take you all the way to the suburbs where you and all the decent people live. But Mbare is encroaching on you inch by inch. Have you ever been in war? I saw one first-hand and it's not a pleasant thing. You see, men like my husband are funny creatures – when they reach a certain age feel they need to revive the excitement that they once had in their younger days. They look at their wife and she has aged, even put on a little weight. They begin to experiment, first with younger girls, then they work their way all the way back to the top until they are screwing their own grandmothers, but they still can't get that excitement. So they do something radical, they become beasts with their experimentation. That's why this country is in the mess it's in because it's being run by stupid men. I hope you're following me so far."

"I am." I was nodding my head throughout her spiel.

"Don't interrupt me. I have ambitions that run to the highest office in the land. My ministry is one of the few functional ones left, because I can get things done. I've bled for this country and dedicate my life to its service. I also have many enemies all around me waiting to bring me down at a moment's notice. The information that you have given would be very useful to them if it falls in their hands. That's why this has to stay in this office and go nowhere else. I need to be able to trust you, Vimbai."

"You can trust me." I shifted in my chair uncomfortably. She flicked through the pages of the journal and began to tear it up. She passed the leaves through a shredder and binned the cardboard covers.

"There now, that's gone. Tell me, how is Chiedza?"

"You mean my daughter Chiwoniso. She's fine."

"That's good. Are you looking after her well?"

"Yes." I was beginning to wonder where all this was going.

"Girl children are very special. They are a gift from God. What school does she go to?"

"Admiral Tait."

"And are you happy with that school."

"The teachers there are very good."

"She'll need to go to a good secondary once she is finished, though. Arundel, Chisipite and Dominican Convent are the ones that spring to mind. The most important thing to me is loyalty. I place a value on it above anything else. Those who are loyal to me, I reward. Those who are not, I punish. Those two things are as constant as death and taxes. This deed you have done for me, I will carry in my heart forever. Wherever I may be you can come to me and ask what you will."

"I understand you perfectly. I swear I will not tell anyone what I know."

"That's the right thing to do. This boy, Dumisani, where is he now?"

"I don't know, he ran away from me after I confronted him."

"Leave this with me. I will take care of everything. You go back to your life, Vimbai. Find yourself a good man, and this time, make sure you know what you are getting yourself into."

Thirty-seven

I walked through the packed streets of the city feeling like I was being weighed down by thirty pieces of silver. People marched in different directions, here a woman carried a basket laden with fruit on her head and there a man with a bicycle pump walked along whistling a tune by Oliver Mtukudzi. In this mass of bodies I wondered if there were others like Dumi hiding in plain sight. A young man with a tight pair of trousers walked past me. Was he one of them or just someone who could not afford to get himself a new pair? Schoolboys with perms walked by; they could be on their first step down that road as well.

I went onto First Street where a street magician was walking on a wire, blowing flames in the air. A crowd had gathered around him, tightly packed together. People no longer feared pickpockets. That profession had died because no one carried a wallet anymore. The bricks of money in my purse would not have enticed anyone, I thought, as I went past Barbours department store with large back-to-school advertisements on the windows.

There was a restlessness in me as I struggled with my conscience. My phone rang but I could not answer it on the street. It was probably Sarah asking after me. I made a note to make her my manager since there was no way I could give the job to Dumi now. I got a lift and headed for Budiriro to see Fungai.

Dropping off at the shops I headed to the open fields where he told me he held his club. I looked all round where once there was bush; people now grew maize. The streets were busy as usual with idle youths hanging about hoping for better times. I stopped one unkempt lad wearing khaki shorts and asked if he knew where the philosophy club was held.

"Of course, everyone knows those lunatics. Go across the field and head for those rocks over there. You will find them talking nonsense there." He went off before I could say thanks; the young don't care.

Once I had cleared the field, I saw a group of ten young men sitting and talking. One of them sat far from the rest. I guessed who he was immediately. Fungai had told me of a chap called Tonderai who refused to brush his teeth as a protest for the way the country was being governed. He occasionally went around different government departments tormenting officials with the shear power of his torrid breath until they would chase him away after they had suffered enough. Fungai had tried to discourage this but Tonderai had persisted, saying he was a disciple of Diogenes the Cynic. Even now among friends he had to sit at a distance and shout his points across because not one of them could bear to be near him. There was a tattered exercise book beside Fungai. It was the handwritten copy of Plato's *Republic*, which he'd painstakingly copied out over a month because he could never hope to have enough money to buy a real copy. Its leaves rustled in the wind and he placed a protective hand over it to prevent it from being blown away. They were engaged in a fierce debate.

"The goodness of man is an inherent quality which resides in his soul from the moment of conception. It's not something that needs to be taught, though its qualities can be nurtured through study and self-discipline," one of them explained waving his hand ferociously in the air.

"But you've not explained why the quality of good is inherent, but not that of evil. I say man has these dual qualities in equal measure and both are desirable at different times during a man's development.

For example during childhood, particularly infancy, it is more desirable to draw upon the good than the evil because if children were evil, society would abandon them. Yet when a man has matured he will use both to further himself and achieve his ends. In old age a man reverts back to solely being good because he needs society to look after him more and does not have the strength to perform evil deeds."

"What do you think, *sisi?*" Fungai said, pointing to me. The others all turned their heads to listen.

"I don't know what you were talking about," I replied, hoping to get out of answering.

"We are trying to discover if the true nature of man is good, evil or something in between."

"The Bible teaches us that we were in a state of grace until Adam sinned and so sin is passed down on all of us unless we repent and we are baptised."

"We try to discover the truth for ourselves here. We do not refer to the Bible as an authoritative text. To us it is just one of many philosophical texts and while we do pay it attention we do not place it on a pedestal." Fungai spoke gently. "I'm happy you've finally come to our club."

"I have to be honest and say that I would not have come if there wasn't a question on my mind for which I can't find the answer."

"Then ask what you will and we'll see if Lady Philosophy might have an answer for you." They looked at me with eager eyes their ears pricked to hear what I was going to ask.

"I want to ask about homosexuality."

The sun was beating down on us on this rocky plane amidst green fields. I sat down with my legs crossed. They were all quiet for a minute until Fungai began.

***

"The question of what the human body may or may not be used for is one that is as old as time itself. The question of what is termed human sexuality, is perhaps even older.

"Before you proceed you must explain what you mean by human sexuality," the one called Munashe asked.

"It is that attribute within humans that makes them interested in sex. Sex being that most pleasurable function of the body, which is sometimes used for procreation but more often not. We assume that there are two types of sexuality since everything is made in pairs, light and dark, good and evil, etcetera. The one we shall call heterosexuality, which is an attraction of opposites, and the other we shall call homosexuality which is an attraction of matching subjects.

"What of bisexuals?"

"Bisexuality is not a true essence in itself because at any given moment in time it can fall into the category heterosexual or the category homosexual. Therefore it is an illusion that misleads us from the truth of our enquiry. And so we will avoid that false detour which will lead us nowhere."

"That is as true as it is necessary."

"So we have defined what is and what isn't but because we have defined sexualities we have to announce that it is males and females who partake in these activities. That men should be attracted to women and vice versa is something we shall take for granted. We now also take for granted that humans are created in these pairs, but there we find ourselves mistaken. There are the hermaphrodites, those born with both genders, who straddle the line between man and woman."

"That can only lead to the conclusion that man and woman may not be as distinct as they seem," said one called Armstrong.

"Correct. When we use our brains, we can see that between the two genders there are a myriad possibilities; the leap from male to female is not as straightforward as our senses tell us. Therefore when you look at what you think is a man and what you think is a woman, you often fail to recognise or acknowledge all the other ambiguous possibilities.

(At this point one of them stood up and left.)

"If there weren't this subtle range of distinctions, then these two sexualities would not exist; there would be one or none but not two genders. At this juncture we must then say that homosexuality is not only there but that it is actually necessary, after all approximately ten per cent of any population is gay or homosexual."

"This is bullshit." (Three more stood up and left.)

"In our reasoning we can only turn to Lady Philosophy. Those who have preconceived notions of where she will lead us must leave because they are not seekers of truth."

(Another two stood up and walked away.)

"What I need to know," I asked, "is, if say I had a friend who was a homosexual and the law is clearly against homosexuality, what should I do?" I was worried that my question had been too bold.

"In a few short steps, we've already discovered that homosexuality is necessary. The question you now ask is of friendship and the law. There are two sets of laws, the 'natural law' and 'man-made law'. The illegality of homosexuality is the product of man-made laws."

"But," I said, "there are things that are wrong in both natural and man-made laws. If stealing falls within both, then why should homosexuality only be covered by one?"

"Stealing is a topic that we can have a day's debate on by itself but we must note that stealing is something that harms other people whereas homosexuality between consenting adults behind closed doors harms no one," Fungai said firmly.

(I wish I could have said it had harmed me and broken my heart. At this point two more stood up and went, leaving only Fungai, Tonderai and myself.)

"I can only say that friendship should rise above man-made laws, which tend to be capricious by their very nature."

***

I could not have known at that time that my question would lead to the collapse of his philosophy club. Whenever Fungai walked the streets with his dogs, youths called him the *ngochani* and kept him at arm's length. Only his friend Tonderai remained with him and even he perhaps only because with his breath he could find no other friends.

Thirty-eight

The phone rang at three in the morning. Its luminescent light brightened my dark room where I had only just managed to snatch my first sleep in many days. I reached for it but my drowsy hand only succeeded in dropping to the floor. It stopped ringing for a few seconds and started up again.

"Hello."

"Why haven't you been answering, I've tried your number nine times now."

"Who's this?" I asked, feeling more dead than alive.

"It's Trina, listen, something very bad has happened to Dumi, he is at the Avenues Hospital. Put some clothes on, I'm coming to get you!" Her voice sounded agitated. She hung up so I didn't get a chance to ask what had happened.

There was a knock on my bedroom door. I answered and Maidei opened it. She looked like a ghost standing in the doorway so I asked her to turn the light on as I swung over the side of the bed and sat up.

"Mama, some men came here this afternoon and they took all the things in Dumi's bedroom. I didn't know what to do. They said they were from the CIO."

"Why didn't you tell me this as soon as I came in?"

"I was already asleep. I only woke up when I heard your phone ringing."

"Go back to sleep," I said, knowing I should have thanked her. I put on a T-shirt and some jeans and went to get myself a hot drink to perk me up. I knew Trina would hoot the whole neighbourhood awake if I didn't come as she asked. Had she really said Dumi had had an accident? At least he was at the Avenues, which was the best hospital available.

No sooner had I fixed my cup of tea than her headlights flashed at the front gate. I walked out, my hair a mess, and wrapped my cloak tighter to keep out the night chill. Dogs were barking disturbed by the noise. I got in and put on my seat belt.

"We've got to hurry because he's in a really bad state." My heart began to pound.

"What happened?"

"He got seriously beaten up. Someone found him in a ditch along Chinhoyi Road and took him to the hospital. He was drifting in and out of consciousness, but they wouldn't treat him unless they had money up front. Somehow, he must have given them my number because they have put me down as his next of kin. Is everything all right between the two of you?"

"How much do they want? There is only so much I can get from the cash machine."

"No need to stress just now. I told them to treat him and I would get the money but they refused to do anything until I coughed up. Can you believe it? He was dying and they wouldn't touch him until they got cold cash there and then. I had to get Derek to rush in, in the middle of the night, with a suitcase full of money."

"I couldn't bring myself to tell her all that had happened.

"It's going to be all right," she said, "they're used to dealing with this kind of brutality. They see it on a daily basis."

I opened the window and a blast of night air cooled my face. Trina was doing eighty in the city and running through red lights. We arrived at the hospital and went straight up the stairs to the ward he was in. This hospital didn't have the smell of death one found at

Parirenyatwa. The floors and walls were clean. The nurse in a white dress told us it was all right to go into his room.

At first I didn't recognise the person lying on the bed in front of me. His head was the size of a football and the face was puffed up so much his eyes could barely open. They had a canister of oxygen beside the bed, which hissed continuously to aid his laboured breathing. I took his hand and began to weep by his bedside. Seeing him like this cut right through my soul.

"I'm so so sorry, Dumi. It's all my fault." The words came out as a whisper.

"I'm just going out to see if the nurses can give me some coffee or something," Trina said. I was sure she was just giving us time.

Dumi let out a groan when I placed my hand on his chest. He struggled to speak but I told him to keep quiet and save his strength.

"Thir-sty" he said. I gave him a sip from the beaker on the cabinet beside his bed. The water spilt down the side of his mouth where dry clots of blood were caked.

"I didn't mean for this to happen. I couldn't have known they would do this." I could not stop crying.

Dumi lay half dead as if waiting for the angel of death to come and take his soul. I could hear a trolley going past, maybe a patient being wheeled from one ward to the other. Trina came back in holding two cups of tea.

"The staff here are very helpful." She gave me one. "He's such a nice guy, I don't know why anyone would do this to him. Maybe robbers perhaps, but to do this to someone is just plain evil."

If only she had known of my involvement, she would have been disgusted by me. Dumi's limp hand lay in mine.

"What did the doctors say?"

"It's not looking too good. There was extensive trauma to the head and that's what they are mainly worried about. His skull is fractured in three places and there's a risk that fluid has seeped in, so when the specialist comes in the morning they're going to do a procedure to relieve the pressure on his brain. Are you going to tell his parents?"

"I don't think he would want them to know."

"Is there something about all of this that you're not telling me?"

I said nothing.

"Fine, keep it to yourself. I'm going home for a snooze; I'll be back in the morning. I'll pass through your house and get some fresh clothes and a toothbrush for you."

I held his hand the entire night, watching his chest rise and fall slowly as if it could stop at any time. I fell asleep in the chair with my head resting on the bed.

The nurse woke me up in the morning and offered me something to drink. I stretched my aching back and gazed on Dumisani all bruised and swollen.

"They'll be coming to take him for the op soon. Maybe you can go home and come back after."

"I have to stay. There's no way I'm leaving his side." It's difficult to stop loving someone, even when they have done something that you once thought unforgivable. There isn't an on off switch for love. I wept for Dumi and hoped that everything would turn out okay. The guilt and the realisation of the magnitude of what I had done hit me hard. When they wheeled him out I spent the morning praying for the Lord to spare his life. I wanted him back home with me where he belonged. I went through his things and found Mr M___'s phone number. When he heard what had happened, he began to sob uncontrollably on the phone. He kept saying he should have protected him and I tried to reassure him that all would be well.

After hanging up, I wondered if what Dumi had said in his journal might be true. If it was, then he had one kind of love for me and another for this man, we were both loved but each of us in their own way. It would be a lie to say I did not want him to myself, but this didn't mean that if I couldn't have him, I would want him dead. Dumi was too nice a person and he'd helped me so much in my life. If only I could find a way of righting things again.

Thirty-nine

The operation went well and he was transferred to the ICU to recover for a time before being brought back to the ward. The days and weeks that followed were some of the worst in my life. The only person I could tell from his family was Michelle. She had to make up some excuse with the family about how Dumi and I were too busy renovating my house for him to go up and see them. That seemed to buy some time. She was a pillar of strength. She paid Trina her dues and handled the near daily demands from the hospital for more money. Sometimes they didn't even have the drugs so we had to rush off and buy them from the pharmacy before they could administer them. We alternated during visiting hours to make sure someone was always by his side. Having been educated in America she understood his situation better than anyone else. Mr M___ also dropped in every so often with flowers and in disguise. I would watch how tenderly he would plump up Dumi's pillows to make him comfortable. I was touched and affronted at the same time.

After a week Dumi regained consciousness and began to speak. I was alone with him when, in a weak voice, he said, "Thank you for looking out for me."

"I'm so sorry for everything." My voice broke.

"It's I who must beg your forgiveness. I should have been upfront with my true intentions for you. There were signals I gave off about us which misled you.You see, for a long time I used to think of my gayness as a cancer for which I needed treatment. Then I met Colin and he told me how wrong I was. Now, I realise it is just something I was born with and as long as Zimbabwe can't accept it, I'd better live somewhere else." When he spoke, his voice was barely audible and only the right side of his lips moved.

"I shouldn't have read your journal in the first place."

"That was meant to be. I wrote it hoping that one day someone like you might read it as an explanation of why things are the way they are. You just found it before it was ready and I was ready."

"Can you tell me anything about what happened?" At this point Michelle walked in. Her face brightened immediately seeing that her brother was able to speak. She sat on the side opposite to me and held his hand.

"After I left your house, I walked into town and booked myself a room at the George Hotel. I was resting there when three men barged into my room and blindfolded me. I don't know where I was taken, but it was to some sort of torture house in the city. They beat me on the soles of my feet. One of them kept saying, "We haven't been told why we're doing this, but we'll fix you." They must have worked on me all day, reviving me with water whenever I passed out. I begged them to let me die and they said I would soon enough. The last time I passed out they must have thought I was dead and dumped me somewhere. There are many gaps in my memory."

The pain on Michelle's face mirrored my own. I know she was wishing she could tell her father so he could find the people who did this, but that was impossible. No one would stand up for a homo who'd been attacked. I phoned Mr M____ and told him the good news.

"Praise God! I'll be there as soon as I can."

He arrived soon afterwards wearing a large farmer's hat that covered his face. Once he was in the room he removed it and went over to Dumi. He gave him a gentle stroke on the face then stopped as if he had suddenly realised that we were there.

"How are you feeling, my boy?"

"Like I've been hit by a truck." Mr M___ laughed nervously.

"I need to know if you are well enough to travel."

"I can if needs be."

"The people who did this to you will come back to finish the job as soon as you leave this place. Consider yourself lucky, they do not usually get it wrong the first time." There was a hint of professional disappointment in his voice.

"This is my home, I will not leave."

"Dumi, listen to him, don't be a foo.." Michelle cried out.

"They will target your family as well if you are trying to resist what it is they're going to do. I've trained men like that in my day. It's best you leave the country and go somewhere where they'll know you will not be an inconvenience to them."

Michelle and I got up to leave the room. A part of me still rebelled, saying that what was happening in that room was against God and Nature, but the love I had for Dumi stayed with me. Michelle and I took some time to walk out amongst the jacaranda-lined avenues, making a few trips round the block. It was a lovely day; the weather was not too hot. Michelle put her arm around me; she understood how much I cared for her brother.

"Ya'll need to go on the Jerry Springer show."

"What's that?"

"Never mind. I know this is a lot for you to take in, and I respect the way you are handling yourself. I don't know what I would do if I was in your shoes." Michelle stopped and we stood in the shade of a jacaranda tree. "I have known for a while now that my brother is gay, and I'm cool with it. The rest of the family isn't. Dumi came out to us just after he finished high school, he wasn't seeing anyone at the time. Dad went ballistic, Patrick wanted to bust his knee caps, it all went crazy. Nothing happened for a year until one of dad's friends mentioned in passing that he had met Dumi on holiday with some white guy. You should have seen my dad howling with rage. To try and protect the family name, dad arranged with his pals in police to have the Canadian dude deported before anyone knew what was up with his son. It was a tough time for Dumi, he has suffered a lot just for being who he is. I want you to know one thing though, Dumi loves you and Chiwoniso more than anything in the world. You guys were family to him, when he had no one. He is just different, in a world which wants to force him to be what he is not. Don't ever stop loving him, he needs you now, more than ever."

When we got back to the room, Mr M___ was standing in a corner his eyes darting about the place.

"We're going to move to the UK," Dumi said. "Vimbai, can you get my passport? And, Michelle, please organise a ticket for this weekend."

I didn't have the heart to tell him that his passport was gone. Everything he owned in this world had been taken away. There was no time to lose; it was Thursday. I said farewell and rushed into town.

When I got to Construction House I was told that the minister had left for the day. I prayed that she would see sense and spare his life.

***

The next day I was up early and waited in the lobby of her office. The security guard recognised me and put me through without a problem. She had meetings in the morning so I had to wait and pace around for three hours. The receptionist, a skinny girl, tried to strike up a conversation, but I was not interested.

Around three o'clock her phone rang and she told me I could go in.

"Vimbai, I didn't think you'd come to claim your reward so soon," she said from behind the stack of papers on her desk. "Do sit down."

"I've come to ask for a favour that you may not approve of."

"And what may that be?" Her eyebrows rose slightly.

"I am coming to ask for Dumi's passport." I interlocked my fingers and pressed hard on my knuckles.

"Tell me, is my husband coming to see that young man at the hospital?"

A thought flashed in my mind, to tell the truth or to lie, which was better?

"He is," I said, and closed my eyes at this second betrayal.

"I knew that already. You see, we know everything. It's good that you didn't lie to me, but tell me exactly why you need this passport."

"I want his life spared, so he can leave the country."

She reached into her drawer and pulled out the green passport. She thumbed through the pages and settled on one.

"It says here that he has a visa to go to Britain. Is that where he wants to go? It should suit him well there. Their government is full of gay gangsters. They even walk the streets parading themselves. He will be happy in Sodom. But there are other things I have to take into consideration." Her face darkened. "Will he keep his mouth shut while he's there?"

"We have spoken about it and I'm certain he will," I lied.

"Are you willing to put your own life down as an indemnity? Such that if he so much as mutters something in his sleep you will be forfeit."

A shudder passed through my body as I nodded my consent.

"I always keep my promises." She threw the passport at me, "Consider us square now. My debt to you is paid in full. When you go to sleep every night remember the consequences of what you have agreed to."

Forty

On Saturday evening Michelle, Dumi, Chiwoniso and I stood inside the lobby at Harare Airport. The stars in the night sky did not burn so brightly that night. There was a queue of people checking in. Some black families with kids who only spoke English in a funny accent – children of the Diaspora. Dumi held himself upright masking the pain in his tortured body. His left side was weaker than the right and doctors had said this was permanent. It was not the Dumi I knew. He looked older and his skin did not have the same glow it used to. His hair was cropped short and there were scars on his scull. We huddled together in a hug. We breathed each other's scent in, perhaps that was the only part of my old Dumi that remained.

"I'm going to miss you both so much," he told us and gave us each a tight squeeze. That was it. The last I saw of him was when he was speaking to the uniformed woman at the security gate. He said something and she smiled. I knew then that the secret which made him the best hairdresser in Harare was that he knew how to make anyone feel like a woman.

He walked up through the gates and vanished out of sight.

***

I received a phone call from him a few days later. He complained about the cold and told me how much he missed me. In the months that followed the calls kept coming but with less frequency. He was settling in well. Mr M___ did not try to go to the UK; his name was on a list of people barred from entering the European Union. He wrote Dumi a long letter apologising and explaining that he had responsibilities in Zimbabwe that would tie him down for the rest of his life.

In a way I will always love Dumi. He restored my faith that there are still some good men out there. I never got to tell him of my deal with the minister because wherever he may be I want him to live his life to the fullest, without fear.